A Pleasant Death

AN EDITH ELLIOTT MYSTERY - BOOK ONE

JAYNE BAILEY

THREE BEES
PUBLISHING

THREE BEES PUBLISHING

Dedicated to the memory of my amazing nan, Edith. I'm endeavouring to keep you alive in my own little way.

Love always Xx

Chapter One

W asn't it strange how quickly your life could change? One minute, you're sitting on a picnic blanket with your friend, Sarah, reluctantly watching a bunch of old age pensioners play a rather laborious game of cricket, and the next, after one rather forceful bat from eighty-year-old Harry Lanscombe, you find you're being rushed off to the nearest hospital after the cricket ball careered beautifully through the air and straight into your head.

Edith had been immediately knocked out, landing face-first in Sarah's homemade Victoria sponge cake, sending a tidal wave of jam and cream all over Sarah. An ambulance had been called, and Edith had been hoisted onto a gurney and deposited into the back of the ambulance before she'd even come around.

She had awoken to the sight of one very young paramedic gently wiping Edith's lips with a wet wipe.

'Am I bleeding?' asked Edith, as she ran her tongue along her lip line. 'Why does it taste like jam?'

The paramedic smiled down at her. 'That's because it is jam,' she said. 'You're lucky you landed head-first into that cake. It broke your fall.'

A pain shot through Edith's skull, and she instinctively reached for her head, only for the paramedic to gently lower it back down again.

'Best not to touch that,' she told her. 'That is most definitely *not* jam.'

Edith lapsed in and out of consciousness. One moment, she was lying down in the ambulance, bumping up and down over the numerous potholes that blighted the UK's roads, and the next, she was in A&E hooked up to all manner of bleeping machines. After several hours, an MRI, thirteen stitches, and various observational reports from the nurses, Edith had found herself being wheeled out of the busy accident and emergency department and onto a quieter and more calmer ward.

The following day, Sarah came to visit her and had bustled through the door the second 10 a.m. had arrived.

'Oh, thank goodness,' she'd blurted tearily. 'I thought you were a goner when that ball ricocheted off your head. Here, I've brought these for you.'

Edith's eyes drifted down to the copy of *Woman's Own* magazine and the cake tin in Sarah's hand.

'You didn't have to, Sarah, but thank you.'

'It's another Victoria sponge, I'm afraid – not the one from yesterday, obviously. That was past saving,' said Sarah, shaking her head sorrowfully. 'But I already had the ingredients in the house, you see. So it made sense rather than go out and buy more. But then, on the bus, on the way over, I suddenly worried that it might be too upsetting for you to have another Vicky sponge. It's not going to bring back painful memories or anything. Is it?'

'Sarah. It was a cake, not a landmine. I'm sure I'll be fine.'

Edith took the cake and the magazine from Sarah's hands and set them down on the empty cabinet beside the bed.

'Harry was in a complete mess, as you can imagine,' continued Sarah as she sat down in the chair. 'He's never actually managed to hit the ball before, so that alone had come as a little bit of shock to him, but then when it hit you, well, that completely took the wind out of his sails.'

She rose again from the chair, went to the cake tin and removed the lid. 'Would you like some?' she asked Edith.

Edith felt her stomach turn. She still had dried cream gluing her hair together in clumps. 'Not just yet, thank you.'

Sarah cut herself a generous slice and started to eat. 'The game was a write-off after that. They've rescheduled it for next weekend,' she continued, sending a spray of crumbs over Edith's hospital nightdress. 'But, Malcolm, you know the one, the health and safety guy, has insisted on a cordon. Now, spectators have to be at least twenty meters behind it. Twenty meters! I may as well watch it from my bedroom window for all the good that'll be.'

Edith had been glad when midday had arrived, and Sarah, with the now empty cake tin in her hand, had left as promptly as she'd arrived.

She tentatively lay back on the pillow and closed her eyes, waiting for the painkillers that the nurse had given her to take their effect. The dull thump inside her skull was beating like a relentless drum, and Edith was thankful that the hospital had placed her in a private ward. She'd heard various shrieks from other patients throughout the previous night. Thank God she hadn't had to share with them.

She stole a glance through the window and watched the nurses dart up and down the corridor. They worked so hard and for such little pay, Edith thought to herself. Who'd be a nurse? Not her. Blood and guts just weren't her thing – she couldn't even watch *Casualty* on television without retching. Even artificial limbs and fake gore managed to turn her stomach. No. Not for her at all. She'd wanted to do something else entirely. But her father had soon put a stop to that: The wretched man. Edith pushed away thoughts of him and closeted them back into the depths of her aching mind. She didn't want to think about him, and his archaic ideologies, and his snobbery, and the annoying way he spoke in that ridiculous, plummy tone. Sir Edward Francis Montgomery Allerton could stay neatly tucked away, thank you very much.

The door to her room opened, and in walked an impossibly tall doctor. He had the trademark stethoscope dangling around his neck and was wearing a pair of shocking red trousers, which clashed horrifically with his light blue shirt. He gave a polite smile to Edith as he pulled the chair closer to the bed and sat down.

'Mrs Elliott. Pleased to meet you. I'm Doctor Harding. You've been in the wars, I see,' he said, pointing at her head.

'I've had better days,' said Edith flatly. 'Doctor. When can I go home? I can't stand being cooped up in here, and apart from a headache, I feel absolutely fine. It's a waste of a bed me being here. I'm sure there are sicker patients out there who need it more than I do.'

Doctor Harding's lips pulled back into a grimace, and he coughed nervously. 'Well, that's why I wanted to come and speak to you. I've reviewed your MRI scan, and I found something which is quite concerning.'

Edith twisted the bedsheets in her hands. 'Concerning?'

He nodded back at her and looked down at the file in his hand solemnly. 'Yes. I'm afraid there's no easy way of saying this. The scan shows that you have a brain aneurysm; quite a sizable one from our point of view – more than 10mm in size.'

He sat silently for a moment, allowing his words to sink in.

Edith's breath caught in her throat. She gave a liberal cough and sat up in the bed. 'From the cricket ball?'

'I don't think so. I think that it was there prior to your accident,' he replied.

'Wh-What does this mean for me?'

The doctor's dark blue eyes softened, the corners of his eyes creasing as he gave a sympathetic smile. 'I'm afraid, given the location of the aneurysm and...your age, surgery wouldn't be an option.'

He continued to tell Edith about the type of aneurysm it was, pointing it out to her on the scan, but the words muffled in her ears. She was, to all intents and purposes, a ticking time bomb – not that the doctor had used those exact words, but still, Edith couldn't help but feel that whether or not it ruptured was in the hands of fate and the gods. She could, as he explained, go on to live the rest of her life without any complications, but there was always that risk that one day it would rupture, and when that happened, it would be unlikely that Edith would survive.

Ten minutes later, the doctor's phone shrilled, and he glanced down at the screen. 'I'm so sorry,' he mumbled. 'I'm being called to an emergency.'

Edith nodded back at him. 'Don't worry. I understand. Thank you for explaining it all to me,' she told him because she wasn't sure what else to say.

After he'd left, Edith had sat silently in the bed, blocking out the outside noises as life around her continued. Was the location of the aneurysm really the issue? Or was it a case that she was too old to risk the expense of surgery? Was her chance of survival lower because she was a pensioner? Her body may have felt seventy-one with her aching joints, but her mind was still as able, as clear, and as young as it had ever been. She gave a heavy sigh. No. The doctor hadn't been lying to her – Edith had a knack for spotting liars. He'd been completely honest and frank with her, if not a little formal, but she wouldn't hold that against him.

She reached for the magazine that Sarah had brought for her, opened it to the first page, and then promptly closed it again. She should call somebody, she supposed. There were her children, Alexander and Charlotte. But Alexander was in Prague on a business trip. Although Edith secretly knew that it wasn't business at all. He was having an affair with a hairdresser called Liberty, of all names! And had taken her away for a dirty weekend rendezvous. Charlotte, her carefree, wild and unpredictable daughter, lived in a commune, or cult, as Edith preferred to call it, and where phones were forbidden. Probably because the 'leaders' didn't want any of their followers to reach out for help when their senses returned. And yet, when Edith had taken a coach and made the long journey down to Exmouth to visit Charlotte when she'd first joined, she'd seen the leader, who went by the rather ridiculous name of 'Master' and found him hiding behind a large oak tree on the grounds with a mobile phone in one hand, and a funny-smelling cigarette in the other. His name, as Edith later discovered after a bit of digging, was actually Albert Pearshouse; a fifty-two-year-old former bus driver who'd left his wife and three children behind in their council house to start up a commune on an old farm which he'd of course purchased using the money of his followers. Albert, or Master, or whatever the hell he wanted to be called, had managed to clear thirty thousand pounds worth of debt and buy a seven hundred thousand pound farm in the space of three short years. It always amazed Edith just how easily people were fooled, but she'd been astounded when she discovered that her daughter was amongst them. She always thought that she'd brought Charlotte up better than that. But maybe Charlotte had more of her father's traits than Edith realised: unthinking, impulsive, gullible. As much as it galled Edith to admit, it seemed that her daughter had inherited more than just Ronnie's green eyes.

In the end, she decided to wait until Alexander had returned home from his illicit tryst before calling him. And Charlotte, well, she'd have to send her a letter to inform her, which would no doubt be opened and vetted by the commune prior to being delivered into Charlotte's hands. So much for free love.

For lunch, the nurse brought her a rather sad-looking and dry jacket potato with a small pot of cheese, a plain yoghurt and an apple. Edith longed to be back in her little council flat and sat in her living room eating something a little more substantial and a damn sight tastier than the measly meal she'd been given. She pushed the jacket potato aside and opened the yoghurt, spooning the bland white mixture into her mouth.

So, she was on the home stretch of life, as it were. How many more Christmas's would she wake up to? How many more bangs of the New Year fireworks would keep her awake until the early hours? Edith wasn't sure. But what she did know was that however many more years she had left in her, she was going to make the very most of them. The second that Edith was discharged from the hospital, she intended to do something that she'd avoided for over fifty years. Her children wouldn't be happy when they discovered the truth. Or perhaps, given the circumstances, they might be? Either way, it wasn't about to put her off. There were many new bridges that Edith was about to cross, one or two which she'd burnt down many years before. The only thing she hoped was that she was strong enough to still cross them.

Chapter Two

Harry Lanscombe folded up his cricket whites into neat little bundles and placed them on the chair, ready for the weekend. It had taken him hours to get the blood mark out of the knee on his trousers, obtained when he'd knelt down next to Edith's unconscious body the other day. He'd have to write a strongly worded letter to the laundry detergent company, who'd declared, according to the advert, that their detergent could remove stains in one wash on and on a thirty-degree setting. Quite frankly, they'd been talking out of their arse on that one. It had taken Harry three washes, with the machine on the last wash having to be set at the dizzying temperature of sixty degrees! He was lucky that the trousers still bloody fitted him. Hopefully, the company would send him a goodwill gesture to keep him quiet. With any luck, they'd send him a complimentary box of the washing power – that stuff cost a fortune. But if they did, they'd better make sure it was the family-sized box. If they tried to fob him off with one of those little ones, he'd write straight back to them demanding they rethink their offering: A second letter highlighting the fact they were ripping off an old-age pensioner usually did the trick.

He merrily whistled his way out of the bedroom and into his little kitchen. Honestly, there wasn't enough room to swing a cat in here, thought Harry as he opened one of only three cupboards the builder had managed to squeeze in there and pulled out a tin of new potatoes. Not many people liked the taste of them, but he'd managed to pay just five pence for a tin when he helpfully pointed out to the shop assistant that they were one month out of date according to the date stamp on the base. As a result, Harry had emptied the shelf of the odd-tasting tinned potatoes into his shopping trolley and had walked away with over twenty tins, which had cost him a little over one pound at the checkout. What a bargain!

What to have with them, though? That was the question. He supposed he could get the frozen battered cod out of the freezer and whizz up a sachet of parsley sauce to drizzle over them. But how much had that fish cost him again? Quite pricey if he remembered correctly; he'd tried to get the cashier to knock the price down, citing the fact that the top of the box had been opened, but the cashier had promptly refused, citing back to Harry that Harry had been the one who'd opened the box when he thought that nobody had been looking. Oh well. You couldn't win them all.

No. Not the fish, Harry decided. Not if he'd paid full price for it. He opened cupboard number two and smiled at a dented tin of corned beef.

'Yes! That'll do nicely,' he said, smiling as he remembered how many times he'd had to 'accidentally' drop the tin on the floor before it was suitably mangled enough to request a discount. How much had he got it for in the end? That was it – a whole fifty pence. Who didn't love a bit of corned beef hash? He'd grown up on the stuff, and it hadn't done him any harm.

A meal for two for less than a pound. Harry beamed to himself. He couldn't understand why everyone was moaning about this cost of living crisis. He hadn't been affected in the slightest. Some people called Harry a tight-arse, but he considered himself to be frugal, or sensible, or not downright stupid when it came to parting with his cash.

Did he need a mobile phone? No. For years, Harry had been content with using the public call box to make phone calls. Granted, that had become difficult now that the council removed the phone box because, apparently, it wasn't being used enough – at all, in fact, apart from Harry. But it hadn't been too much of a bother to knock on Elsie's door in the flat below and ask to use her phone when he needed to. And Elsie didn't mind, or at least Harry thought she didn't mind, but she had been answering the door less and less recently even though Harry could quite clearly hear *Loose Women* blaring out from the television in Elsie's living room.

Did Harry need the heating on all day and night? No, of course, he didn't. His electric blanket did the trick, and it only cost him pennies to run as opposed to the hundreds it would set him back to use his central heating. Sure, his bones ached a little more, especially when the weather dropped perilously close to zero, but if he popped on an extra jumper and huddled further down under the electric blanket, he was absolutely fine.

It was the same with the electricity. For the vast majority of the time, Harry would quite happily sit in darkness with only a candle beside him for light. It was a little antiquated, he supposed, and sometimes he felt like Wee-Willy Winky holding his candle as he made his way to bed, but it was a

damn sight better than having the flat become Blackpool
illuminations. He allowed himself to boil the kettle once
a day, and that was always in the evening for his cup of
cocoa. And using the toaster? You could forget about that.
It made Harry's head spin faster than his electricity meter
did when he used it. Those things should be outlawed for
the amount of electricity they guzzle.

Not tonight, though. Tonight, Harry had a guest, and
he had to pull out all of the stops with this one. Maybe he
should go with the fish after all? You never got a second
chance to make a first impression, so his dear old mother
used to say, God rest her soul. Yes. Definitely the fish for
tonight's guest.

He placed the tin of corned beef back in the cupboard
and retrieved the fish from the freezer, sliding the two rigid
pieces out onto a baking tray. He turned on the oven and
baulked at the noise as the fan spun inside. How much was
it going to cost him to cook everything tonight? He mused,
but then he quickly pushed the thoughts away.

What was the point in worrying? If tonight went to
plan, then by the end of the weekend, he wouldn't have
to think about money for a long time. It had been a while
since he'd done this, and his coffers were running dry. He
just needed to top them up a little bit more to keep him
going.

What a weekend he was going to have! If he batted another bowl like he had the other weekend, then his team would win for sure. It was a shame that Edith had gotten in the way last time. She always seemed to like to poke her nose in and ruin things for people. Well, maybe next time, she'd think twice about sitting so close to the game. Not that he'd actually have to worry about that this time, thinking about it. Malcolm had insisted on the marquee being erected for this match. It only usually made an appearance for May Day or the summer carnival, so it was quite a treat for everybody. Felicity from the café was setting up a small stall providing coffee and cakes and the like, much to Sarah's disgust, who said that you needed to take a mortgage out to buy one of Felicity's Belgian Buns, but it had already been arranged with the committee and they could hardly back out now.

Brian, the landlord of the Ewe and Lamb, was also setting up a minuscule bar in the far corner of the marquee, so with any luck, Harry might find himself having a pint of bitter or two being bought for him if he managed to whack another ball like he had the last time.

Yes. This weekend was going to be amazing and one which Harry would remember for a long time.

Suddenly, the doorbell shrilled, and Harry bustled, tucking his shirt neatly into his trousers and straightening his tie.

'Showtime,' he whispered to himself as he went to answer the front door.

Chapter Three

The ageing solicitor peered over his glasses and narrowed his eyes.

'I must say, Mrs Elliott. It was quite a surprise when I received your letter. It's been such a long time since I last saw you. I almost didn't recognise you, but now, looking at you, I can see a touch of your father in you.'

Edith winced, resisting the urge to hurl abuse at Anthony Morgan at his unintentional insult.

'Yes. Well, unfortunately, it seems the passing of time hasn't been kind to me if that's the case,' she replied flatly.

Anthony Morgan had been a junior partner of the law firm when he'd first started working for her family. He'd managed her father's affairs and estate with all of the excitement and enthusiasm of a Labrador puppy, and

Edith had been surprised to find that despite his ailing years, he was still very much involved with her family. In fact, she'd been astounded – not just that he was still practising law but merely the fact that he was still alive. He was at least twenty years older than her, but it appeared that his decision to still work had more to do with her than she'd realised.

'When you first went missing, back in that blistering heatwave in 76', I'd been tasked with discovering your location. Your father had been a formidable man, as I'm sure you know. There had been no expense spared, and I remembered promising him that I'd find out where you'd gone before the end of that week,' he took off his little round spectacles and rubbed at his eyes. 'A foolish thing to say, really. You'd gone to great lengths to hide away. Great lengths, indeed. It had never occurred to me that you might have changed your name. Now, it's far easier to track people, but back then, everything was paper documents, and we just didn't have the manpower to go trawling through deed poll records. But I didn't want to give up on you – I couldn't. I had to know that you were okay. '

'My father must have been furious,' said Edith.

Anthony Morgan heaved himself up from his chair and shuffled over to an old wooden filing cabinet. It gave an angry squeak as he opened the drawer, and he delved his hand inside, retrieving a yellowing file.

'You know better than anybody just how tempestuous your father could be. We used to call him Jekyll and Hyde – you never knew which side you were going to get that day. Most of the other junior staff refused to work with him.'

'He was a pig-headed bigot,' replied Edith.

He smiled at her, revealing a row of crooked tombstone teeth. 'It would be unprofessional of me to agree,' he replied. 'But I will say that the fact that both you and your mother...how shall I say it? Absconded? Well, it didn't go unnoticed by the staff here. We saw just what a difficult man he was.' He half opened the file and then closed it again, pausing momentarily before continuing. 'Did you ever find her? Your mother, I mean. I did look, but much like yourself, she just vanished. I did wonder over the years whether or not you'd planned this together.'

Her beautiful mother. The stunning, elegant woman who sashayed around the ballroom at dinner parties. The woman who'd woken Edith up each morning with a 'Good morning, sunshine' as she pushed back the heavy curtains, letting the light illuminate her bedroom. The woman who plastered on a smile as thick as her make-up every day to conceal the bruising that hid beneath. The tortured soul who walked on eggshells around her father. The woman who'd lost her voice and her identity the second she'd said 'I do' at the wedding ceremony. Edith had never blamed her for leaving. But she had blamed her for leaving her and her brother behind at the mercy of their father.

'No. I never saw her again,' replied Edith. 'There was no great conspiracy between us. She left, and that was that.'

If only it had been as simple as she made it sound.

The solicitor gave a solemn nod and reopened the file. 'A mystery in itself then. Maybe one day we'll get to the bottom of it all.' He coughed noisily as the dust motes from the file danced their way through the air and into his mouth. 'Right. To business, as it were. So, your father did make provision for you in his will. It came as quite a surprise when he decided to change his will. It was all so last minute when he summoned me to Althorp Hall that winter morning. He passed away not long afterwards. I suppose in our later years, we start to question our past decisions – try to make good our wrongs.'

Edith, frankly, couldn't give a tinker's toss about her father's reasoning. When she'd seen his obituary in the newspaper, she hadn't felt a single morsel of sadness. She'd been glad that he'd passed away. She'd also ignored the repeated advertisements calling for her to come forward to claim her inheritance. She'd wanted nothing to do with the man. Not his money. Not his name. And most certainly not his affection.

'I've obviously kept a keen eye on your inheritance over the years. Your brother, thankfully, refused to have you declared legally dead and insisted that I employ a financial advisor to manage your share of the estate as effectively as possible. And I'm pleased to say that those investments have most certainly paid off over the years. Granted, there were some financial hits in the eighties and then again in 2008, but happily, it didn't make too much of a dent. You, Ms Allerton...forgive me, I mean, Mrs Elliott, are now worth a considerable sum of money.'

Edith leaned towards the desk. 'How considerable are we talking?'

Anthony Morgan smiled back at her. 'Around twenty million pounds worth of considerable.'

***

Edith had decided to travel back home by taxi – not a standard Uber either. She'd hopped into an expensive black Hackney carriage, not paying any attention to the quickly rising fare metre as it clocked up pound after pound for the journey back to her flat.

The money had been a bittersweet compensation payment from her father from beyond the grave, and although Edith had known she'd inherited something, she never imagined in her wildest dreams it would have been as astronomical as that. Just wait until she told Ronnie.

'Was it worth it?' Anthony Morgan had asked her just as she was about to leave his office. 'Was it worth walking away from your family, all in the name of love?'

Edith thought back to the handsome man she'd met back in 1973. He'd been one of the many gardeners who tended to the land on their estate. Ronnie Elliott, when she first met him, was lean, muscular, and rugged. He had the hands of a worker, calloused and rough, not at all like her father's with his soft, unblemished skin. Ronnie had wooed her, whispering sweet nothings into her ear and presenting her with bunches of roses he'd plucked from the numerous bushes on the grounds.

Up until meeting him, Edith had led a sheltered life. She'd attended an all-girls school, and apart from the odd interaction with local boys at the village shop, her father had taken every possible step to shield his daughter from anybody he deemed undesirable. But he hadn't factored in the copious amount of staff who worked for him in their grand home. And although the vast majority had remembered their station in life, it appeared that Ronald Elliott was not one of them.

She thought back to their secret rendezvous in the walled garden behind the tennis court and how they'd sat on the grass and cuddled as Ronnie regaled Edith with all of the wonderful things that they were going to do when they were an official couple. She remembered the smell of the flowers he'd given her. The touch of his hands on her skin as he gently rubbed her arm. And then, she recalled the furore their relationship had caused when it was discovered thanks to a rather nosey kitchen maid who'd immediately rushed to tell her father what she'd seen. The fury of her father. The name-calling and accusations. The way she'd been locked inside her bedroom. How Ronnie had been immediately sacked. The way he'd climbed up the drainpipe outside her bedroom window in the middle of the night to organise their escape. The way they'd rushed across the grounds under the cover of darkness, hand in hand, and spent their first night together in a bed at a B&B they'd stopped at on their way to Birmingham. The impromptu wedding just six weeks later. It had all been so romantic back then. Or so Edith had thought. But within months, their new reality kicked in. Ronnie struggled to find work and they lived off the little bit of money that Edith had managed to save before she'd left home. Their flat was a small, dingy hole above an Indian takeaway restaurant which stank permanently of spice. She remembered the arguments. Ronnie staying out until all hours, stumbling through the door, reeking of booze. She remembered him being in and out of work. The hunger that twisted in her stomach when they didn't have enough money to buy food. She remembered the pain when she went into labour with Alexander and then again two years later with Charlotte, giving birth alone as Ronnie went to the pub to 'wet the baby's head'.

'Yes. It was worth it,' she lied back to the solicitor. 'I wouldn't change a thing.'

An hour later, Edith walked through the door to her flat.

'I'm back, Ron. You're not going to believe what I've got to tell you,' she called out as she took off her coat and hooked it over one of the pegs in the hallway.

She went straight into the kitchen and filled the kettle with water and returned to the living room as she waited for it to boil.

'You'll never believe how much money I've got, well, we've got...no, actually, me – how much money *I've* got.' She was babbling. Edith always babbled when she was excited. 'Over twenty million pounds! I have to be honest, I'm sort of questioning my principles now I know how much is there. Just think of all of those years when we didn't have a bean to our names, and all the while, there was that huge wedge waiting there. Principles never put bread on the table, did they?'

She looked over at the fireplace at the urn. The urn remained motionless.

'I know. I can't believe it either,' she said. 'It's astounding, isn't it? And I was right; it was the same solicitor from all of those years ago. He still works at the firm. You'd have thought he would have retired a long time ago. I mean, he must be in his nineties.'

Still, the urn remained motionless.

Edith couldn't quite recall the first time she'd started talking to Ronnie in the urn. Actually, if she was being factually correct, there was only half of him in there. The other half had been sucked up by her Dyson vacuum when she'd accidentally knocked the urn off the mantlepiece, sending Ronnie dust all over her carpet. But Edith had struggled with being completely and utterly alone for the first time in her life. She'd always had people around her: Her mother, brother, her father, the staff at Althorp Hall, then Ronnie, Alexander, Charlotte, and even Charlotte's daughter, Sunbeam, or Sunny, as she preferred to be called nowadays. Every second of every day, Edith had always had company, and to find her suddenly faced with only herself had been too much for her to handle at the time when Ronnie passed away.

Initially, she'd only spoken the odd word here and there. And that transcended into a sentence. Which eventually transformed into an entire conversation. It had felt odd at times, speaking to a jar filled with human ashes. But it had helped when Edith had stuck two googly eyes to the front of the urn; she didn't feel completely mad if the jar had some human features. She did toy with applying a mouth with a Sharpie pen but quickly discounted it – after all, she didn't want to look mad if anybody spotted it when they visited.

The kettle clicked off in the kitchen, and she went back to make herself a cup of tea. 'What's that?' she shouted towards the living room. 'Oh, I know exactly what I'm going to do with it,' she said, smiling as she squeezed the teabag against the side of the cup, She added the milk and returned to the living room. 'I'm going to do exactly what the hell I want.'

The urn and its googly eyes stared back.

Chapter Four

Winston Mayhew rubbed away the smudge on the lens of his binoculars and held them back up to his face. They were his trusty, old army issue ones that he'd never handed back when he'd been discharged, one of the few perks he'd had when he'd left the army – that and his army pension, which certainly made his life much more comfortable than most pensioners he knew. Oh, and his old service revolver, which he'd also failed to hand in. The army back then was a different entity from the one that existed now. Paper records were easily lost, and with so many guns lost in action following the Second World War, it had been easy to pack them away in his suitcase and carry them out of the barracks on the last day of his service.

His head first drifted up to the branches of an old oak tree in the corner of the green, his lenses settling on a magpie nest. Had the eggs hatched yet? he wondered, but seeing no movement, he lowered his sight onto the marquee that had been put up in preparation for the cricket match on Sunday. Winston adjusted his position in the bushes, careful not to rustle the leaves too much for fear of bringing attention to himself, and smiled as Sally Marston, the wife of the pub landlord, Brian, and her ample cleavage, came into view. She was wearing a rather revealing low-cut top that day as she helped heave heavy crates of beer inside the marquee. Winston had never seen her wearing that before – it must be new.

He took a quick cursory glance at the other people milling around as they helped set up and tutted.

'Not much doing today, Dickens,' he said to the sleeping Beagle at his feet. He was such a good dog, Winston thought to himself. He was an old boy, much like himself, and although he loved a walk, Dickens would happily fall asleep when Winston found a good viewing spot, allowing him to get on with his voyeurism without drawing attention to the fact that somebody was hiding away and spying.

Winston sighed and slid his binoculars back into the case, which dangled on a strap around his neck. 'Come on, fella,' he said, giving Dickens a gentle nudge with his foot. 'There's no point in staying here. Let's get back, have our dinner, and then we can come out again later tonight.'

The dog gave a squeaky yawn and reluctantly stood up. Winston attached the lead to the dog's collar and then, as quietly as he could, made his way out of the bushes, checking that there was nobody around to see him emerge on the footpath that lined the main road.

Winston couldn't remember the first time he'd started to use his binoculars for something other than bird watching. It was definitely after Mabel had died; he knew that much for certain. He'd have never done anything like that when she'd been alive. But unfortunately, his beautiful wife had passed away some ten years before, and with nobody else in his life to keep him company, and if he was being honest, no chance of finding new love, Winston had found himself with a lot of time and his hands and no way to fill it.

When he'd first stumbled across the binoculars tucked away in the back of his wardrobe his initial intentions had been to use them to sit quietly outside and observe nature in its everyday glory. But after a while, he'd discovered nature was as unpredictable as it was boring. You never could count on the birds to make an appearance when you wanted them to, and it was during one of these lulls where

Winston was waiting for something to happen that he'd inadvertently seen movement in one of the windows of the houses that backed onto the park.

As he adjusted the lenses, the blurriness cleared, and the new couple who'd moved into Sunflower Cottage came into view. They were in one of the bedrooms upstairs, and at first, it was clear that some kind of argument was afoot. The man was pointing an accusing finger at the woman; his face flushed red as he raged silent words across to her. The woman, in response, promptly burst into tears, and the man, clearly guilt-ridden at having made her cry, rushed to her side and began to comfort her. He kissed her face gently, and then, within seconds, Winston's eyes widened with shock as they began to kiss passionately and rip each other's clothes off. He watched until they'd dropped out of view of the window, and then a flustered Winston had quickly packed up his things and hurried home. He never did find out what their names were.

His trusty little spy tool had provided Winston with so much pleasure over the years. Not just in the sexual sense, but in a way, it had made him feel as though he was somehow involved in somebody else's life other than his own. He'd been secretly privy to so many juicy little scandals, so many secrets, that Winston had found himself with an arsenal of information which would make the Sunday tabloids look tame.

Take dear old Harry Lanscombe, for example. Everybody thought that he was a sweet old man when he wasn't smashing old ladies' skulls in with cricket balls, that is. But Winston knew better. He knew just what type of man he was – he'd seen hundreds of the same over the years. If only people knew! He wished he could tell somebody, but in order to do that, he'd have to admit how he'd found out, and that could land him in a whole heap of trouble. So, for now, at least, Harry Lanscombe's secret was safe with him.

But Winston would blurt it out in a heartbeat if he thought he could get away with it.

Chapter Five

Thankfully, the weather was being kind to the UK for once, and the village had reached the dizzying heights of fifteen degrees, which wasn't bad at all considering the time of the year. As a result, many of the residents had been taken over by a sense of community and had ambled to the green to watch the cricket match – and undoubtedly take advantage of the outdoor bar. Somebody had even organised a burger van to set up next to the marquee, and the air was thick with the smell of onions.

Edith was sitting at a small fold-away table, on a wobbly chair in the marquee with, now that she was rich, a glass of prosecco – well, she didn't want to draw attention to herself sipping Champagne now, did she? Sarah was sitting opposite on a mismatched chair to hers, which was considerably lower; her prosecco that Edith had so generously bought her remained untouched.

'What's wrong?' asked Edith, nodding at Sarah's glass on the table. 'I only got it because you said that you loved the stuff?'

Sarah slid the glass closer to herself. 'I'm just all in a kerfuffle. I offered to bring some cakes along to sell, but Felicity managed to pip me to the post, and now she's selling her overpriced rubbish and making a tonne of money. Have you seen the state of her jam tarts? If you can call them that. There's barely any jam in them at all. And don't get me started on her cinnamon swirls.'

Edith took another sip and wrinkled her nose. God, it was dry stuff, prosecco. Give her half a lager and lime any day. Maybe she'd get herself one after this?

'I wouldn't worry yourself,' she told Sarah. 'At least you'll be able to enjoy the match, not like Felicity. Look at the state of her. The poor love is rushed off her feet.'

'Yeah. But at least she'll have made enough money in one day to pay her rent at the end of the month.'

Edith furrowed her brows. 'Are you saying you haven't got the money to pay your rent?' she asked, guilty thinking of the eight-figure balance in her bank account.

But Sarah waved a dismissive hand. 'No. Nothing like that. It's just that it would have come in handy. Especially considering we've got our annual coach trip to Bournemouth coming up.'

Bournemouth? Forget Bournemouth. Edith had been pouring over brochures for Caribbean cruises.

Just then, Harry Lanscombe entered the marquee, and a small cheer went up amongst the rest of the team, who were already on their second pint of beer.

'Here he comes, the bruiser batsman,' shouted Allen Berry, spilling beer all down his white jumper. 'You'd better watch yourself, Edith. We don't want you getting in the way again.'

A round of cheers and guffaws bounced off the marquee's panels, and Edith smiled, raised her glass to the 'hilarious' Mr Berry and wondered how many of her stitches would pop if she walked over to him and headbutted him.

Harry, buoyed up from his new-found fame, strode confidently over to the table and set down a glass of clear liquid in front of Edith.

'An apology offering,' he said, pushing the glass towards her, and Edith smiled her thanks. 'I'm glad to see you're back on your feet. I'm truly sorry for what happened last weekend.'

'No need, Harry. Accidents happen,' she told him. 'Good luck with the game.'

'Not that'll you'll need, I'm sure,' added Sarah sweetly. 'You've got the luck of the devil.'

Harry gave a bashful look. 'Well. Here's hoping,' he replied, and he trundled out of the marquee and over to the pitch to ready himself.

Edith pushed away the remaining prosecco and picked up the drink Harry had bought for her. She sniffed at the rim of the glass. What had he got her? Gin? Vodka? She couldn't tell, so she took a sip and immediately grimaced.

'What's the matter?' asked Sarah. 'Did he get you a double measure or something?'

But Edith shook her head. 'No. The tight old goat got me a glass of water.'

***

At what age should men stop playing cricket? thought Edith.

It had been a long and extremely slow game, and given the age of the players had resulted in several unscheduled breaks. At one point, the umpire had even requested an oxygen tank be brought for Malcolm Healy because the eight-six-year-old was wheezing so heavily that he was worried the old man might drop down dead at any moment.

Edith had lost interest in the game over two hours ago. She had no idea which team was in the lead, who had scored what runs, and indeed, even how many runs had been, well, ran. She'd remained firmly rooted on her wobbly chair and, after the pungent prosecco had been drunk, had opted for her favourite lager and lime drink from the bar. She was on her fourth glass, which probably wasn't wise considering she was still taking painkillers for her head, but at that moment in time, she'd rather die of accidental overdose than boredom.

The teams were currently having yet another break, and Sarah had buggered off to the toilets twenty minutes ago and hadn't returned. Edith had spotted the long queue to the plastic port-a-loo snaking around the edge of the pitch earlier, so good luck to Sarah with that one. She'd be another twenty minutes at least.

Felicity, having completely sold out of stock, had temporarily closed and hurried back to her café to see if there were any other cakes tucked away in the kitchen which she could sell. That woman must have made an absolute killing today, thought Edith. Well done to her.

Harry was sitting on a stool at the makeshift bar, sipping on what Edith guessed was a glass of water. Harry, after such a promising start the previous weekend, had failed miserably this time around. He'd peacocked his way over to the wicket to a roar of cheers from the crowd, readied himself and his bat into position, braced himself as the nimble Arthur Studley bowled the ball at the speed of light, and visibly deflated as the ball sailed straight past him and smashed into the stump behind. Suffice it to say, everybody had stopped buying poor old Harry drinks. His fifteen minutes of fame had been just that.

Suddenly, the game and the day itself, it seemed, came to an abrupt halt when a sudden April shower began to fall. Small soft droplets of rain bounced off the taught marquee roof until, within minutes, they had transformed into heavy globules that pounded against the material like a drum. The small tent quickly filled with people, keen to seek shelter from the rain, and Edith found herself surrounded, hemmed in like cattle waiting for slaughter. Even the air became moist as the rain, the damp ground, and the heat from the bodies wafted around inside like an ominous, heavy fog. To make matters worse, there was the unmistakable stench of armpit, and Edith wondered how long it would take for the shower to pass so that she could get her mildly drunken behind out of there and go home.

As it transpired, it was ten long and sweaty minutes. And with the rain finally easing, the people in the tent began to leave, and Edith felt as though she could finally breathe again. She picked up her handbag from the floor, hooked it over her shoulder and left with the throng. That was enough for today. She'd stop by the chip shop on her way home and pick up a nice piece of cod and chips with mushy peas on the side for her and Sarah – and not the small ones. She'd treat them both to a dolphin-sized portion of cod because why not?

Edith had barely stepped outside of the marquee when a piercing scream penetrated the air. Everybody stopped and turned to look at one another. And when the scream shrilled for a second time, Edith found herself, along with others, hurrying around to the back of the tent.

There, they found Felicity Horsfall screeching at the top of her voice. Scattered around her feet were jam doughnuts, blueberry muffins and chocolate eclairs, and beyond that lay the body of Harry Lanscombe. His eyes were wide with surprise, unblinking and staring at the heavens above. There was a large wound on his head, blood dripping down to the grass blades underneath, and next to his head was a cricket ball caked in his blood and hair.

Chapter Six

DCI Simon Jackman winced as the tyre of his Jaguar jutted into a large pothole in the car park of the Ewe and Lamb pub.

'Bloody hell. I only had the tyres replaced the other week,' he bellowed.

'You should have looked where you were going,' DS Emma Hooper replied nonchalantly from the passenger seat as she flicked through her Facebook feed on her mobile phone.

Simon's mouth set in a thin, grim line. 'I did look,' he said through gritted teeth. 'I thought it was just a puddle. I didn't realise there was a pond hiding underneath it.'

'Never trust a puddle. Not with the state of the roads today,' Emma replied. She pressed the like button on one of her friend's posts, and a chirpy beep sounded around them. She closed her phone and dropped in her handbag by her feet in the footwell. 'It's not the sort of place you'd expect someone to be murdered, is it?'

Simon looked out of the car window and took in the rows of neat Edwardian houses, the litter-free pavements and the neatly trimmed hedges. It was a far cry from most of the murder scenes they'd attended before: inner-city turf wars, seedy backstreets, and the occasional drunken brawl outside a busy nightclub.

'It takes all sorts, I suppose. And in my experience, most murders are rarely planned. It tends to be a spur-of-the-moment thing. So, technically, anybody could be a would-be murderer.'

Emma raised a quizzical eyebrow. 'Even you?'

'At this precise moment in time, especially me!' he replied, wondering if his car tyre was deflating as they sat there chatting. 'Come on. Let's take a look and see what we've got.'

They got out of the car to a sea of hushed voices and curious glances. The pub's beer garden was overflowing with people who'd attended the cricket match and intermingled with a swarm of uniformed police officers who were taking all of their details. They strode across the road to the field, where a few of the locals huddled together at the side of the police cordon. Beyond that, Simon could see a marquee poking out from in between the branches of the trees. As they approached a PC nodded at them and lifted the plastic police tape for them to pass through to the crime scene.

As crime scenes went, Simon thought it was all very pleasant. A lush green field dominated the area, where the scattered remains of an abandoned cricket match cast an eerie backdrop. The whole field was lined with mature trees and hedges with small clusters of daffodils and tulips dotted around their roots. The birds tweeted merrily from their nests. The sun was shining brightly, casting shafts of light on the ground. There was a sweet smell of onion drifting from the burger van where a small queue of officers stood placing their orders or tucking into an oversized hotdog. Inside the marquee, there was a makeshift cake and coffee stand and a small bar in the opposite corner. If Simon was ever to be unfortunate enough to be murdered, he hoped that it was somewhere just like here.

He looked over at Emma, who was gazing longingly at the few remaining giant-sized cookies at the cake stand. 'Diet going well then?' he asked her.

'Don't ask,' she replied. 'I'm perfectly fine until I see food.'

They went back outside and went around to the back of the marquee, where a small army of forensic officers were strategically examining the area and the body.

'Don't come any closer,' instructed one of them, looking Simon and Emma up and down with disdain at their lack of protective clothing.

Simon peered over his shoulder and looked down at the body on the ground. 'What have we got? What do we know?' he asked.

'One male. His name is Harry Lanscombe, according to witnesses. Blunt force trauma to the back of the head with what appears to be a cricket ball, although I'll have to confirm that back at the lab. Preliminary investigations seem to indicate that the attack took place where the body was found.'

Simon turned to Emma. 'Seen enough? Or do you want to get togged up and take a closer look?'

Emma shook her head. 'No. I've seen more than enough, thanks.'

'First thoughts?' asked Simon.

'Well, I've gone right off that cookie.'

'About the murder, I mean.'

She rolled her eyes. 'I know. I was only joking,' she let out a heavy sigh. 'As much as it pains me to say, it's like what you said earlier. I'd say this was an impromptu attack. An argument gone wrong, perhaps? Although, I can't see why anybody would want to fall out with a pensioner.'

'Don't let age fool you. Pensioners can be the most stubborn and rude people on the planet,' said Simon as he turned and walked back out of the marquee, with Emma following behind. 'I once had a great aunt who was arrested for child cruelty.

Emma's eyes widened. 'Arrested? What did she do?'

'She used to be the go-to babysitter for the family. She had no kids of her own, so most of my family would pay her when they needed one of their kids looking after while they were at work, or if they went out for the evening. There was one of the children that she took a particular dislike to, no idea why. She just hated him. And the second the parents waved them goodbye and drove off, she'd tie him up and lock him in a cupboard for hours on end – no light, or food, or toilet breaks. Just let him sit there for hours, alone and frightened.'

Emma let out a whistle. 'Jesus! That's terrible. What happened to the kid?'

He looked over and gave her a wry smile. 'He grew up and became a DCI for the Police Service.'

They made their way back to the pub and spotted one of the new detectives, DC Aaron Phillips, who'd recently been assigned to the team. He was young – still in his twenties, for God's sake. But what he lacked in experience, he made up for with a natural intuition and endless enthusiasm.

'Phillips,' said Simon as he approached. 'What can you tell me?'

DC Phillips consulted his notebook. 'The victim's name is Harry Lanscombe – eighty years old. Lives alone in a flat, 78B Joiner Road. Known locally as the resident tight-wad. Somebody mentioned that he has a child who he doesn't have anything to do with. They don't know the reason why, so that might be worth looking into more. But other than that, he doesn't have any known enemies, and he hasn't fallen out with anybody, so at the moment, it's all a bit of a mystery.'

'Who found the body?' asked Emma.

DC Phillips looked down at his notebook again. 'A Felicity Horsfall – local café owner. She's sitting over there on that table.'

DC Phillips pointed to the beer garden, and Simon's eyes followed his finger until they settled on a red-eyed, snuffling woman sitting at one of the tables. There were a few people who sat with her, comforting her.

'Let's go and see what she's got to say,' said Simon, motioning for Emma to join him, but he was stopped when PC Phillips grabbed his arm.

'Before you go, Guv. There was one thing that somebody mentioned. It just sounds like gossip if you ask me, but it's always best to mention it, seeing as Mr Lanscombe's head was stoved in with a cricket ball.'

Simon narrowed his eyes. 'Go on.'

DC Phillips took a step closer to Simon and lowered his voice. 'This cricket match started last weekend but was called to an abrupt halt when Harry Lanscombe batted a corker of a ball. Apparently, it flew across the pitch and smashed straight into the head of a woman. She was knocked unconscious and ended up being taken to hospital. It caused quite the hoo-hah.'

'What's this woman's name?' asked Emma.

'Edith Elliott, and she's sitting right next to Felicity Horsfall now. Like I say, it might be nothing, but you never know.'

Simon looked over at the table again and took in Edith Elliott. She was a slight woman, possibly no more than eight stone. Salt and pepper grey hair, fashioned neatly into a short bob. She didn't look like a stereotypical pensioner, with her smart haircut, blue jeans, black top and deep blue blazer jacket. But as Simon had learned over the years, you should never judge a book by its cover, especially when it comes to murder.

'Good work, Phillips,' said Simon. 'Keep me informed if anything else comes up,' and then turning to Emma, he said. 'Come on. Let's get over there and see if we can unravel what's gone on here.'

Chapter Seven

As preliminary interviews went, it had to be the most sedate and polite one that Simon had ever encountered in all of his career. So far, the pub landlord, Mr Brian Marston, as he discovered his name to be, had brought over a pint of bitter and a ploughman's lunch for Simon and Emma. Another resident at the table, Sarah Winslow, kept calling them Dearie and Petal and had offered to bake them both one of her 'famous' red velvet cakes and bring it to the station for all of their hard work. Malcolm Healy, the self-appointment health and safety expert, had given them a complete incident report of the day's events in shockingly precise chronological order. And Felicity Horsfall, through her blubs and generous nose-blowing, gave them a clear and concise version of events that led to her finding Harry Lanscombe's body.

'I'd gone back to the café to pick up some more cakes, you see,' said Felicity. 'We'd totally sold out and only had a few cookies left,' Felicity cast a smug look in Sarah Winslow's direction. 'I'd only been gone fifteen minutes or so – not long at all. And as I was walking across the road, back towards the marquee, I thought I heard somebody call out my name from behind the tent. So, I went there, and that's when I found him.'

A fresh wave of tears trickled down Felicity's face, and she buried her head in an oversized handkerchief supplied by the ever-resourceful Malcolm Healy.

So far, the only person who hadn't offered any input was Edith Elliott, who'd sat mutely listening to the details of the others, narrowing her eyes occasionally and staring into space as though her ageing brain was trying to make sense of what everybody was saying.

'And what about you, Mrs Elliott?' said Simon. 'Can you tell me where you were when this event took place?'

A small smile ghosted her lips as though she was secretly pleased with the attention. These old dears always liked it when somebody asked their opinion, thought Simon.

'I was in the marquee. I'd been there all afternoon,' she replied.

'And you never left at all?' asked Emma.

Edith shook her head. 'No. I have the bladder of a camel, thankfully, which came in especially useful after I saw the queue for the port-a-loos. Poor Sarah was stuck there waiting for ages. Weren't you, Sarah?' said Edith, looking over at her friend.

Sarah gave a vigorous nod of the head. 'Ridiculous. It was almost half an hour, I think,' said Sarah, eyeballing Emma as she made a note of what she'd said.

'And did you see Mr Lanscombe at all?'

Edith nodded. 'Yes. He came over to our table and very generously brought me a glass of water, which I didn't drink because, well, it was water. After that, he went out of the marquee and onto the cricket pitch. The game started, and it continued off and on. He came back inside just before the heavens opened. He was sitting at the bar having a drink. And then when it rained, the tent filled with people and I didn't see him again. Well, not until Felicity screamed, and we all hurried around the back and saw poor Harry on the ground.'

'I understand that there was an altercation between you and Mr Lanscombe the previous week?' asked Simon, eyeing her response carefully.

A hush descended on the table and those around them on neighbouring tables in the beer garden, and

Simon slowly glanced around to find that everybody was watching the proceedings.

Edith straightened herself on the chair. 'No. I don't believe there was an altercation.'

Simon spotted the edge of irritation in her voice. And Edith spotted him, spotting it.

'There was, however, an *accident*,' she added, enunciating the last word. 'Mr Lanscombe batted a rather forceful ball, which veered off its trajectory somewhat and ended up slamming straight in the side of my head.'

'That must have been very embarrassing,' said Emma.

'No, it wasn't embarrassing. But it was very bloody painful,' said Edith, drily.

'But still,' continued Simon. 'You must have been extremely annoyed at Mr Lanscombe?'

Edith's eyes darted between Simon and Emma. 'Oh dear. You seem to be barking up the wrong tree, DCI Jackman. I can assure you that I held absolutely no ill feelings towards Harry over the incident. It was unfortunate, granted. But if you'd ever watched Harry play, you know without a shadow of a doubt that it wasn't deliberate on his part. He was terrible at cricket. The fact that he hit the ball was a pure fluke.'

'He was pretty awful at the game,' agreed Sarah, giving Edith a supportive squeeze of the shoulder.

'Total shit,' somebody else shouted over at Simon from another table.

'And on that note,' said Simon, quickly rising to his feet. 'We'd better be on our way.'

He motioned for Emma to follow, and she jumped up off her seat and dropped her notebook in her handbag. 'Thank you for your time,' she told them.

'Are you at the station tomorrow?' said Sarah, looking hopefully at them.

Simon looked over at her with concern. 'Why? Is there something you'd like to discuss with us in private?'

Sarah gave a soft chuckle. 'Oh no, Dear. I just wanted to make sure that you'll be there for when I bring over my signature red velvet cake. Honestly, I think you'll love it. It's not like anything you get in the shops – that stuff is readymade cake mix,' she shot a look of disgust over at Felicity. 'Whereas mine is properly homemade.'

Simon strode off back towards the car, leaving Emma to explain to Sarah Winslow that, given they were investigating a murder, it would be unlikely she'd find them at the station the following day. Simon heard the dulcet groan of Sarah's disappointment drift over the ether, and he let out a loud sigh. God, he thought this was going to be such an easy case to solve. But as it stood, the victim had been surrounded by a group of rather charming, if not mildly annoying, OAPs. Nobody was aware of any ill-feeling towards Harry Lanscombe. Nobody had heard anything. Nobody had seen anything. And to make matters worse, the antiquated villagers had informed him that there was no CCTV in their village because they'd vetoed it during a vote two months previously in the village hall because they were worried that it might ruin the village's aesthetic.

He pulled out a packet of cigarettes from his pocket, took one out and placed it between his lips. He'd told himself that he was stopping smoking that day – something which he told himself most days. But today, just like all of the other days, he needed it. He patted his pockets down for his lighter and tutted when he realised it wasn't in either. He unlocked his car, reached inside and took his spare lighter from the centre console. He pressed down on the button, and the flame flickered into life, but as he drew it closer to the tip of the cigarette, it suddenly extinguished under the hearty blow of somebody standing next to him.

'Don't start on me, Emma. It's my first one of the day,' he said, not bothering to look round at the phantom lighter blower. 'I'm just stressed that we've got nothing to go on. This place is like the village of the damned, if you ask me.'

'That's a tad rude,' he heard a voice say that was most definitely *not* Emma's.

Simon spun around and saw Edith Elliott staring blankly back at him. 'That's a filthy habit. And if you haven't had one all day, then I'm sure you could take it a bit further and not have one at all.'

Simon took the cigarette out of his mouth and slid it back into the box. 'Can I help you, Mrs Elliott?'

'No,' she replied flatly. 'But I can certainly help you.' Edith checked her surroundings before taking a step closer to Simon. 'We may not have CCTV, but we do have Winston Mayhew. Perhaps you might want to have a word with him. He's well known for keeping a close eye on things here in the village.'

Simon raised an eyebrow. 'In what way?'

'In a way, that means he's hiding in bushes and behind trees with his binoculars,' whispered Edith.

'So, in a completely illegal way,' said Simon.

'Yes. He's been doing it for a while. And he was here this afternoon – I saw the bushes rustling on the far side of the pitch, and at one point, his dog, Dickens, popped out the side and relieved himself against the daffodils.'

'Anything else?' asked Simon.

Edith opened her mouth to say more but was halted when Emma returned to the car with Sarah Winslow babbling beside her.

'And I'm quite good with piping, too. Last month, I made a beautiful birthday cake for my niece's daughter – what does that make her to me? My second cousin? Oh, never mind, that doesn't matter. But I piped three huge beautiful roses on the top. It really did look spectacular. Didn't it, Edith?'

Edith gave a wide smile to her friend. 'It was amazing,' she agreed. 'You're a total artisan.'

'Grandniece,' interjected Emma, looking down at her phone. 'Your niece's daughter would make her your grandniece.'

'Shall we?' Edith said to Sarah. 'It's been a long day. We really should be going home. You do have our addresses, don't you, detective? Should you need to speak to us again?' She held Simon's gaze, and he gave her an all-knowing nod.

'Absolutely, Mrs Elliott. Make sure you both get home safely.'

The two women strolled arm-in-arm along the country road, chatting as though they hadn't a care in the world, let alone seen a dead body.

'What do you make of her?' Simon asked Emma, his eyes fixed on the old ladies until they turned the corner and went out of view.

'Well,' said Emma, blowing out her cheeks. 'I'm not sure. I just hope her cakes taste as good as she makes out.'

Chapter Eight

Edith had just waved Sarah off at her doorstep and was making the short walk back to her flat. Her mind, having seized to a stop for so many years, was suddenly filled with an abundance of thoughts and theories. Edith was giddy with the excitement of it all, and then she whipped the thought away again – a man was dead with his head smashed in, after all. Maybe she should show some restraint or, at the very least, a little compassion.

But compassion for Harry Lanscombe was a difficult one, unfortunately. Edith had heard the stories, of course. His persistent skint-flinting had been legendary in the village for many years. Lorraine, the shopkeeper of the local Shop & Save, had told Edith that she'd caught him several times smashing produce in order to get a discount.

She'd been on the verge of reporting him to the police for criminal damage and fraud when Lorraine made the cardinal sin of leaving out a chicken tikka sandwich in the chiller section that was one day past its sell-by date, and Harry had threatened to inform the Environmental Health Department that Lorraine was selling spoiled food. Something which might have resulted in an investigation and a possible extortionate fine unless Lorraine agreed to overlook Harry's tin smashing and fruit bruising in the shop – and also let him have the chicken tikka sandwich for ten pence.

And then there was Brian Marston, the pub landlord. Everybody knew that he and Harry had frequent arguments, the latest being just last week, owing to the fact that Harry had ordered the tomahawk steak and chips, the priciest item on the pub menu, demolished the whole plate within half an hour and even picked up the bone and gnawed on it like he was in the court of Henry VIII, only to then demanded a refund because he'd found a hair on his plate. Brian, all too aware of Harry's penchant for penny-pinching, had re-checked the pub's camera and saw Harry plucking out his own hair and placing it down on the plate. Brian refused the refund, and chaos ensued, with Harry loudly shouting across the bar that Brian was a charlatan and a slum landlord. Brian had flown from behind the bar with clenched fists towards a startled Harry, who, up until that point, had never been confronted before. Glasses were smashed, women screamed, and insults were hurled between them. Thankfully, a full-on punch-up was stopped by the regulars who'd held Brian back, and Harry had beat a hasty retreat out through the old wooden doors of the pub to the shouts of Brian telling Harry that he was barred for life from entering the Ewe and Lamb again.

That was two viable suspects right there, thought Edith. It was a shame that she didn't have the chance to pass on the information to DCI Jackman, but hopefully, the detective guessed that she might have more to say and took the hint when she mentioned having her address.

She was buzzing inside in a way that she hadn't felt for years. For as long as Edith remembered, all she ever wanted to be was detective – not just a lowly WPC who, at least in her younger days, did nothing but admin, but a proper, fully-fledged detective who saw the bodies and organised the raids and who interviewed the suspects. But her controlling father had soon stopped that from happening when he'd found out. After he'd suitably ridiculed her first, of course. Edith had thought that when she and Ronnie had eloped, things might have been different, especially in the early years when they so desperately needed money. But Edith hadn't realised just how controlling Ronnie was either. She'd missed all of those little warning signs, all of the red flags that the younger generation seemed to call it nowadays, and by the time she realised that she'd married a carbon copy of her father, it was all too late to do anything about it – especially after the children came along.

But now Edith was free. She was free to talk to anyone she wanted to, to go wherever she wanted, and most importantly, she was free to not just think how she wanted to think, but free to act upon those thoughts without having to think about what anybody else might think.

She rounded the corner and stopped dead in her tracks. Parked on the road outside was a flash, bible-black Bentley Continental. The pristine paintwork glistened in the setting afternoon sun. She didn't know anybody who could own such an exclusive car as that, and as Edith passed, she took a cursory glance through the blackened rear windows but saw nothing but darkness and her own reflection staring back. She continued the short walk up the path and to the communal front door when she suddenly heard the slam of a car door. Edith turned and raised her hand to her face to shield her eyes from the glare of the sun.

'Hello, sister mine,' she heard a shadowy figure call out, and Edith's heartbeat quickened.

She slowly lowered her hand and squinted as the silhouette neared until, finally, her eyes adjusted to the person standing in front of her.

'Hello, Branwell,' she said breathlessly.

They stood in awkward silence. Somewhere in the distance, a dog was barking, and further beyond, the church bells began to peal for evensong. Branwell let out a long sigh.

'For goodness' sake, Muriel. It's been almost fifty years since we last saw each other. The very least you could do is invite me inside for a drink.'

***

Edith had taken her brother inside, up the stairs and into her flat.

'How wonderfully bijoux,' he said without a hint of irony as he stepped through the front door and into the long, thin corridor.

As flats went, it was small, but for once, the local authority had done a decent job in the design stakes. Off the corridor to the left was the bedroom, small but perfectly sufficient for Edith, and further along, the living room, which boasted two large windows that flooded the room with light. On the right side of the corridor was a minuscule bathroom and, after that, a tiny kitchen.

She led Branwell straight into the living room, but even with her back to him, she could sense him gazing into the other rooms as he passed. He sat down and sank into the sofa cushions.

'Not quite Ming,' he said, nodding at the urn with googly eyes on the fireplace.

She walked over and turned the urn around. 'What would you like to drink?' she asked him.

He was a far cry from the twenty-year-old she'd left behind when she escaped from Althorp Hall in 1976. Gone was his smooth baby-like skin and jet-black hair, but beneath the wrinkles and sunspots, his green eyes blazed like jade, and his wonky smile was still very much wonky but with newer, ruler-straight teeth.

'Do you have any whiskey?' he replied.

Edith shook her head. 'I have Tetley tea or Nescafé instant. Or,' she added, seeing her brother's grimace, 'there is the cooking sherry?'

Branwell bustled and smiled. 'Perfect. Make it a large one.'

She returned a minute later with the glass of sherry for him and placed it down on the coffee table.

'I assume it was Anthony Morgan who told you where I was?' she asked.

He picked up the glass, gave it a quick sniff, and then took a large gulp. 'Who else, Muriel? He said that you're welcome to sue him but added that he'll probably be dead by the time it gets to court.'

'My name's Edith now. Muriel stopped existing a long time ago,' she replied curtly.

'Of course. I'm not sure why I didn't think to check if you were using one of your other names. Mother and father did like to heap them on a bit, didn't they? Although, I think you got the better end of the deal than I did. Muriel Edith Penelope Allerton isn't quite as much of a mouthful as Branwell Atticus George Allerton.'

She gave him a warm smile. 'No. I suppose you're right.'

He took a second gulp from the glass, and Edith could tell that her brother was doing everything in his power not to retch – he could be kind like that.

'I'm always right,' he told her. 'In the same way that I knew you hadn't died. I knew here,' he patted his chest, 'that you were still alive and kicking. Refused to declare you dead. Did you know that? Of course you knew that, Anthony would have told you yesterday.'

She lowered herself down and perched on the edge of the chair. 'How was father after I left?'

'I'd love to say that he was bereft, but you knew our dearly departed father better than anybody,' said Branwell. 'He was furious. Full of hate, and accusations, and general nonsense.'

'How did he die?'

'Oh, you know. Full of regret and in considerable pain. Couldn't have happened to a nicer person.' He let a low chuckle and polished off the remaining sherry in his glass. He stood up and went over and stared at the photographs that adorned the walls. 'Are these your children?'

Edith went to his side. 'Yes. That's Alexander there,' she said, jabbing a finger at a photograph Alex had printed off for her of him on a skiing trip. 'And that's Charlotte, looking rather morose because she'd just discovered her husband had been having a six-year affair with a woman whose morals were looser than her knicker elastic. And this is Sunny, Charlotte's daughter. Her real name is Sunbeam, but she threatened to decapitate us all if we ever called her by that name again.' Edith paused and looked over at Branwell. 'And you? Did you ever marry and have children? What was life like for you after I left.'

He gave a quick shrug of the shoulders. 'I'm afraid to say that I followed in your footsteps. Father caught me in a rather compromising position with one of the kitchen staff.'

Her eyes widened. 'What was her name?'

'Albert,' he replied bluntly. 'Oh, don't look so surprised, Edith. I'm shocked you didn't guess.'

'I was an innocent back then. So, no, I had no idea whatsoever. I bet that went down well with Father?'

'Like a lead balloon with a basket filled with bricks. He disowned me, obviously. Cut me off financially for over thirty years. And to be honest, I had the time of my life. I emigrated to America and lived in sunny San Francisco for much of that time. But then the old man had his first stroke, and sort of summoned me back. I don't know; maybe being faced with his mortality made him sentimental in some way. And I was broke, living alone after another failed relationship, and so I just came back. Strange, really, all things considered. But I won't pretend that the money didn't come in handy. Stayed at Althorp until the old man popped off. The latter years really weren't a bind at all.'

There was a teary sheen on his eyes, and Edith rubbed his arm gently, but he turned abruptly and retrieved his glass. 'I wouldn't say no to another glass of dishwater,' he said, offering it to her.

Edith took the glass from his hands and went back into the kitchen. She was just pouring the sherry into the glass when the doorbell sounded.

'I'll get it,' declared Branwell, hurrying down the corridor, and Edith smiled. She'd missed him and his quirky self. She shouldn't have stayed away from him for so long, but when she'd left, she'd sworn to herself not to drag her brother into it. If her father thought that Branwell knew where Edith was, he'd have gotten it out of him one way or another. She heard a mumbled conversation from the front door, and she turned to see her brother standing in the kitchen doorway.

'Well, well, well, sister dearest. Just what on earth have you been up to? Apparently, this detective,' he thumbed behind him, and Edith saw DCI Simon Morrison peering over Branwell's shoulder, 'wants to question you about a murder.'

Chapter Nine

I t had been a little cramped in the living room. When they'd downsized from the draughty old council house to the compact flat, they'd gotten rid of their family-sized sofa and bought a new, more size-appropriate suite that was more in keeping with their limited space. A two-seater sofa and a solitary armchair seemed a good idea at the time, seeing as the children had left home and they rarely had visitors, but that evening had shown her that perhaps they should have opted for the three-seater all of those years ago.

Branwell, already spotting the potential problem, had quickly dipped past the detectives when Edith suggested they go into the living room and had taken possession of the armchair. Edith and DS Hooper were huddled closely together on the two-seater, and DCI Jackman, ever the gentleman it appeared, had opted to stand in front of the fireplace in a rather manly stance. She'd offered them drinks.

'A quick heads-up,' interrupted Branwell. 'The cooking sherry is top-notch.' But the detectives politely shook their heads, and Branwell gave a nonchalant shrug. 'Oh well. More for me, I suppose.'

Edith told the detectives everything she knew about Harry, from his miserly attitude to his fallings out with Lorraine at the Shop & Save and Brian, the pub landlord.

'Maybe that's why he brought us over the pints and the ploughman's lunch? He's trying to sweeten us up?' suggested Emma, looking up at Simon, who gave a quick shake of the head with wide eyes back at her in response.

'Let's not jump to any conclusions now, shall we?' came his curt reply. 'Mrs Elliott,' he continued, glancing over at Edith. 'Do you know if Mr Lanscombe had any family? A wife? Sisters? Children?'

But Edith shook her head. 'As far as I know, Harry's wife died some years ago – cancer, I think it was. But that was before he moved to the village. I've never heard him mention any relatives, and I've certainly never seen anybody, but then he did live on the other side of the village.'

'Sex. Money. Revenge,' Branwell blurted out. 'It's usually always the motive for murder. Maybe there was a secret lover tucked away in the shadows? Or perhaps, this publican, what was his name? Brian! That's it. Had taken particular offence at Harry scalping himself and planting it on his food?'

'And the money motive?' asked Edith. 'Harry didn't have two beans to rub together.'

But Branwell gave a quick wave of his hand. 'Pah!' he said, dismissing her comment. 'I find that the more money a person has, the tighter they are.'

He gave her an all-knowing wink, and Edith felt her cheeks flush. She wasn't tight! Far from it. Edith had only learned of her substantial inheritance yesterday. What did Branwell want her to do? Splurge it at the casino the second it hit her bank account?

'Have you spoken to Winston Mayhew yet?' Edith quickly asked, keen to veer the subject away from money.

But DCI Jackman shook his head. 'Not yet. But he's on the list.' He flipped his notebook closed and slid it back into his pocket. 'Thank you for your time and for the information. You've been extremely helpful, but we should leave you and your brother to enjoy the rest of your evening.'

He moved towards the living room door, and DS Hooper, Edith and Branwell all stood. Branwell held out his hand towards the detective.

'An absolute pleasure meeting you. Edith is very astute at this sort of stuff, you know. Wanted to be a police officer herself when we were younger. If there's anything else you need to know, please feel free to call again, Simon. Can I call you Simon?'

DCI Jackman looked back at Branwell. 'No,' he said sternly. 'DCI Jackman works just fine for me.'

Branwell gave an unconcerned shrug. 'Whatever you want, detective.'

Edith showed them to the door, waved them goodbye and went back into the living room to her brother.

'Were you flirting with him?' she asked as she plumped up the cushions on the sofa. 'You really have no shame. They're investigating a man's murder.'

'A horrible man by all accounts. He had it coming to him from what you've said.'

'Don't be so unfeeling, Branwell. He meant something to someone, I'm sure,' she retorted.

He let out a loud scoff. 'I bloody doubt it. There's more to him than meets the eye, I assure you.'

He went into the kitchen and placed his glass in the sink. 'It really has been wonderful seeing you again,

Muriel...sorry, I mean, Edith. I've missed you so very much,' he said with his back to her. 'I am glad that I've found you again. Even if it is at the end of our lives.'

Edith's thoughts went to the aneurysm tucked away in her brain. Should she tell Branwell? Of course, she should tell him, she decided. But not today. The past week had been a whirlwind of the unexpected for her: From dying to millionaire, from sleuth to sister. The events had swept her up off her feet and transported her from one emotion to the next. She didn't know what to think anymore. Everything tasted so bittersweet, as though it had all come that little bit too late in her life.

'You're very quiet,' said Branwell, interrupting her thoughts. 'Haven't you got anything at all to say?'

Edith gulped down the golf ball of emotion stuck in her throat and coughed. 'Yes. Thank you for not declaring me dead.'

***

They'd ordered an Indian takeaway in for dinner. The events of the day had left Edith too exhausted to cook, but her stomach growled angrily, reminding her that she hadn't eaten a single thing all day. They'd tucked into a chicken Balti each and shared the keema naan, which was about the size of a small child when she unfurled it out of its plastic wrapper.

With the cooking sherry bottle empty, Branwell had to make do with glasses of water, much to his disappointment. And they'd sat in the living room, plates on laps, and tucked into the food while watching *The Masked Singer* on television.

'That's Sir Ian McKellen. I'd stake my life on it,' said Branwell enthusiastically as he jabbed a curry-covered knife at the screen.

'Branwell. Try as I might, I just can't see Sir Ian McKellen dressing up as a giant luminous green squid and belting out a rendition of *You Sexy Thing*,' Edith said, smiling.

'Fair comment,' he replied as he shovelled another forkful of chicken into his mouth.

Edith swirled her fork around on the plate and stared off into the distance. 'I wonder if the detectives have spoken to Winston Mayhew yet?'

Branwell pulled a face. 'I don't think those two know their arse from their elbow. I mean, they didn't pay any attention to what I was saying about motive even though I know for a fact they're the main reasons for a person to commit murder. It's so obvious.'

'Is it?' she replied, looking over at him.

Branwell nodded. 'Oh, Edith. What happened to you? You were always so good at working things out. Do you remember the time when you discovered a discrepancy in the kitchen books and figured out that the chef was using the Althorp account to fill up her freezer? Or what about the time you launched a full-scale investigation into Hartley, the butler and all because you had a hunch that he was up to something? And it turned out that he was selling the family's rare book collection on the black market.'

'Yes. I remember,' agreed Edith. 'But that was obvious. It doesn't make me special.'

'Sister, darling, you were thirteen years old!'

She tore off another wedge of naan bread and popped it into her mouth. Oh, those wonderful days of youth, thought Edith. When all she had to worry about was whether or not her father would be lingering around the house that evening or slinking off to his club instead to meet up with one of his many mistresses It was always nicer when he wasn't around to ruin their fun.

'That was a long time ago, Branwell. Things have changed over the years.'

He wiped up the remaining curry juice from the plate with some of the bread, popped it into his mouth and then proceeded to suck the end of each finger.

'Just because things have changed doesn't mean it has to stay that way,' he told her. 'There's nothing to stop you from doing what you want now – especially now! You're as rich as Croesus. Your children have flown off. And Ronnie, well, he's somewhat indisposed,' he said, pointing at the urn.

'I don't think they accept pensioners on the payroll at the Police Service, Branwell.'

'True,' he replied, pushing himself up off the armchair. 'But you don't have to be a detective to *be* a detective. We can just do it ourselves. You know what I mean? What do they call them? Armchair detectives...that's it.'

He disappeared into the kitchen with his plate, and Edith heard the tap running as he cleaned it and placed it in the drainer.

'We?' she said when he returned to the living room.

He held out his palms. 'Why not? It's not like either of us has much to keep us occupied, and I always loved it when we used to spend time together.'

Edith looked down at her plate, mulling over what he'd said. It was true she and Branwell had always got on well, and they had made an excellent team. But that was almost fifty years ago. Would it still be the same now that they were old? And with so much time having passed between them, did they even know each other anymore?

'Look. I can see that you're undecided. Why don't we just have a little dabble? You know, go and see what this Winston whatshisname has got to say for himself? We could just make some discreet inquiries and see how we get on?'

She looked over at her brother and sighed. He was six foot three inches tall, broad-backed, and his opinions were louder than the colour ties he wore – there was nothing remotely discreet about him. But, she mused, just imagine what it might be like. It would be like she'd stepped into a time machine. Would it be fun? Undoubtedly. Would it be dangerous? She certainly hoped so. Would she still be any good? There was only one way to find out. Her stomach swirled with the thrill of it all.

'Okay. Let's take a look at it tomorrow,' she replied, giddy with excitement.

Chapter Ten

Simon sighed and glanced down at his watch. He'd told Emma to be ready to leave at ten o'clock, and yet here he was, waiting at the side of her empty desk. They had a tremendous amount of work to get through that day and had scheduled interviews for much of the day, with Winston Mayhew and Brian Marston at the top of their list. Mayhew was due to arrive at any minute.

Simon should have been used to it by now. Emma hadn't been on time once in all of their years working together. When she'd first been assigned to him as his partner, Simon had welcomed the fresh-faced, enthusiastic, and quite attractive detective. He'd been single for such a long time that it had felt nice to have her sitting next to him in the car. Not that Emma had ever looked twice at him –

A PLEASANT DEATH 77

not that he could blame her; she was almost fifteen years his junior after all, and Simon had learnt from an early stage that he just wasn't her type. Still, it was nice to have her sitting in the passenger seat of his car. He even enjoyed the occasional looks he got from other drivers when they peered through the windows as they sat waiting at the traffic lights.

When Simon's third marriage had ended in yet another failure, he'd vowed that he was giving up on dating and relationships in general. Yes, at the ripe old age of forty-five, Simon had called quits on women, and quite publicly too, but now, three years down the line, he was starting to regret his decision. He should have least kept an open mind to casual sex – something which seemed to have worked perfectly well for Mrs Jackman the third, whose persistent affairs had caused the breakdown in their marriage.

He patted his stomach and felt the bulge of his extended waistline. Perhaps he should go on a diet and get himself back on the dating scene. Every single person he knew appeared to be registered to some type of dating site or other, and it wouldn't harm anyone to see what fish were still in the sea for him, swimming around circles waiting for him to dive in.

He still had his hand on his stomach when Emma finally scuttled through the doors.

'Good call. Thinking about going on a diet?' she said, nodding at his stomach.

Simon subconsciously sucked in his tummy and held his breath.

'No,' he replied a little too forcefully. 'My stomach was grumbling, that's all.'

Emma shot him an unconvinced look. 'It's probably grumbling with all of those pastries you keep feeding it. I keep telling you that you should do Keto. It's amazing. Those extra pounds will just fall off.'

Simon held his belly in even more and picked up the file from his desk. 'You're late...again. What's the excuse this time?'

'Believe it or not, I don't wake up looking like this,' she replied, pointing a finger at her face. 'It takes work. Trust me. And it seems to take longer and longer the older I get.'

'You're only thirty-three,' he replied drily.

'Exactly. So it's all downhill from here. Who's first? The pervert?' she asked him, taking the file out of his hands.

He shook his head with frustration. 'We don't know that he's a pervert, Emma. You shouldn't make assumptions.'

She placed a hand on her hip and shot him a look of disbelief. 'Erm. Anybody who skulks around in bushes for hours on end with a pair of binoculars is most definitely a pervert.'

'We only have Mrs Elliott's word for that, so we shouldn't go jumping to any conclusions just yet,' he reminded her.

'Yeah, alright, Sherlock. Let's get this party started, shall we?'

Winston Mayhew sat opposite them in the interview room and stared back at them like a startled fox in the headlights.

'You understand that this is just an interview, Mr Mayhew. You're not under arrest. We'd just like to ask you some questions about yesterday,' said Simon.

The old man fumbled with his fingers and nodded back at them. 'Yes. I understand.'

'I'd like to talk to you about yesterday afternoon and what you possibly saw,' continued Simon.

Winston leaned down and ruffled Dicken's behind the ear. 'Is this going to take long? He's an old boy, you see, and I wouldn't want him to have any accidents.'

Dickens looked up at Winston, yawned and then lay down on the floor, curling himself into a little semi-circle.

'I think he'll be fine,' said Emma. 'So yesterday? What time did you arrive?'

'Arrive? I wasn't there yesterday,' replied Winston.

'We have a witness who can place you there, Mr Mayhew,' said Simon bluntly.

Winston's eyes went from Simon to Emma, down to Dickens, and then back to Simon. 'Whoever told you that is mistaken. I wasn't there.'

Emma slammed her hands on the table, and Simon suppressed the urge to groan at her 'bad cop' routine.

'Listen, Mr Mayhew. We have it on good authority that you frequently lurk,' Emma paused, letting her choice of words sink in, 'in the bushes. Apparently, you like to take in the sights. You're there for most of the day with your binoculars. Now, we're not suggesting that you were involved in the murder of Mr Lanscombe, but it is possible that you might have seen something. Something which you might not have thought important. But if you did, it's your *duty* to inform us. We don't want to have to look into your activities any more than is necessary. Now. Mr Mayhew, let's start again, shall we? Is there anything you'd like to tell us about the events of yesterday at the cricket match.'

There was a lengthy pause, and Simon held his breath – not for the purpose of deflating his stomach this time.

'No. Nothing at all,' Winston Mayhew said defiantly.

They'd ushered Winston back out of the station just

twenty minutes later after Dickens cocked his back leg at the side of the table and relieved himself against Simon's shoe.

'You shouldn't have gone in so hard on him,' Simon told Emma. 'He's ex-army. He knows how to keep schtum when he thinks he's in danger.'

Emma shrugged. 'We should have thrown the book at him under the Sexual Offences Act. How's the sock?'

'Squelchy,' said Simon. 'I think I'll go to the toilets and take it off.' But just as he turned to leave, he saw Brian Marston being led into the interview room. 'Never mind. I'll do it afterwards,' and they went inside and closed the door.

'So, you're saying that you weren't angry at Mr Lanscombe?' Simon asked Brian.

'No,' said the pub landlord, rubbing his eyes. 'I said that I wasn't angry enough to kill him.'

'But you were angry with him?'

'For the love of...yes! I was angry at the man, but I'm not about to smash his skull in over a hair on a plate. Listen, the man was a chancer. He tried to shirk out of paying for anything all the bloody time. We knew what he was like, and we got wise to it. I barred him from coming into the pub, and that was enough for me. And anyway,' he added, smiling back at them. 'I've got three dozen witnesses who'll confirm that I was behind the bar at the time old Harry was killed. I got there in the morning, set up the bar, and I didn't walk out of those doors again until after Felicity started screaming.'

He leaned back in the chair and folded his arms across his chest, pleased with his answer.

'But you didn't have to walk through the doors at all, did you, Mr Marston,' said Emma. 'It was a marquee, not a jail cell. The panels are made of fabric. Who's to say that you didn't just pull one of them back when everybody was distracted and slip out of the back?'

'And who's to say that I did? Did anybody see me do that? Not bloody likely,' he replied smugly.

Simon let out a heavy sigh. This was getting them nowhere fast. 'Interview terminated at 11:45 a.m. Unless you have anything to add? Do you have any questions for us?'

Brian Marston looked up thoughtfully for a moment, and then his eyes settled back on Simon.

'Yeah. I do, as a matter of fact. Why does this room stink of piss?'

Chapter Eleven

Edith looked over the top of her teacup at Branwell, who was currently directing all of his charms onto Winston Mayhew's dog, Dickens. Branwell hated dogs. He'd always hated them, or at least he always had hated them when they'd been younger. So either Branwell had done a complete about-turn, or he was currently trying to schmooze his way into Winston's good books. Edith calculated that it was probably the latter.

'What a lovely boy you are,' he said as he rubbed the dog's stomach for the fifteenth time.

Dickens, loving the unexpected attention from the equally unexpected stranger who'd turned up on the doorstep fifteen minutes earlier, wiggled excitedly from side to side, exposing his generous tackle to everyone in the room without a hint of shame.

'I've always wanted a dog,' lied Branwell, sitting back up in the armchair, much to the dog's disappointment. Edith clocked her brother, rubbing the palm of his hand on his trousers, and smiled to herself.

'So, you were telling us about the interview. Why, exactly, did they call you in?' asked Edith.

Winston's face crumpled with fury. 'Somebody lied and said that they saw me at the cricket match.'

'Gosh. That is disgusting. Why would somebody say something like that?' said Branwell.

'I'd say it was somebody who was trying to put the police off the scent. Criminals do that, you know. They blame other people – other *innocent* people,' fumed Winston.

'But the police weren't suggesting that you had anything to do with the murder, surely?' said Edith.

'No. They weren't saying that. But they did suggest that I was...I was...oh. Never mind. I don't know exactly. It was just their tone. Especially the female detective. She was extremely aggressive, you know.'

Winston's eyes drifted down to the side of the armchair, and Edith followed his gaze to a pair of binoculars. Winston coughed loudly and scurried over to his dog. He knelt down next to Dickens, who, clearly thrilled of receiving yet more fuss, resumed his ungentlemanly position on his back with his legs in the air. As Winston fussed the animal, Edith spotted him push the binoculars behind the sofa, safely out of sight. The second that the deed was done, Winston stood back up and went back over to the living room window.

'I felt that she was a little forceful yesterday when they came to see Edith,' said Branwell and Winston's back stiffened.

'They came to interview you? Why?'

'I think they're interviewing everybody who was in and around the tent at the time of the murder. It's standard procedure,' she replied, silently cursing Branwell for bringing it up. There was an art to sleuthing that her brother needed to learn. 'That's why I came to see you. They told me that somebody had informed them of your presence at the cricket match, and they wanted me to confirm whether or not I'd seen you too,' lied Edith, and she saw Winston instantly relax. 'I told them I hadn't, of course.'

'Good show, Edith,' bustled Winston. 'At least I have you on my side.'

'Winston, old chap,' interrupted Branwell. 'I don't suppose I can pop to your loo? That tea has gone straight through me.'

'Of course. It's up the stairs, second door on the right,' he said, and Bramwell nodded and disappeared out of the room.

The dog jumped up on the sofa next to Edith, knocking her tea out of the cup and straight into her lap.

'Dickens! You naughty boy,' admonished Winston, and the dog's ears lowered against his head. 'I'll just go and get something to clean you up.'

'Oh, no. Don't worry about me,' started Edith. 'Honestly, it's only a little spillage. I'll be fine.'

Winston looked down at the ominous damp patch in Edith's lap and shrugged his shoulders. 'If you insist,' he replied and then proceeded to lecture Edith on the etiquette of dog training.

Edith nodded eagerly, praying that she looked convincing, but she was completely on edge. Branwell was currently mooching through the upstairs rooms in Winston's house and the last thing she needed was for them to be caught out. She looked over at Winston as he animatedly explained how he'd chosen Dickens from the litter of puppies because he had been the only puppy who hadn't jumped up him when he'd first gone to view them.

'Yes. He just sat at the back of the crowd, as it were, and looked up at me. His little tail wagged slowly, and those beautiful brown eyes of his sort of begged me to choose him. It's really quite a marvellous thing to witness,' he continued, and Edith nodded her head more whilst looking over his shoulder to check the time on the wall clock. Branwell had been almost five minutes, and if he didn't return soon, then no doubt it'd be noticed by Winston.

A further five excruciating minutes later, Branwell finally returned looking rather flushed and out of breath.

'Apologies. We had a curry last night, and it went right through me. You might want to give it five minutes before you go up there,' he said to Winston, who wrinkled up his nose in disgust. 'Anyway, Edith. Shall we make a move? I really don't feel too good at all.'

Edith stood up and passed her empty teacup over to Winston. 'Thank you so much. I wouldn't worry too much about the police. I'm sure everything will right itself in the end.'

And before Winston had time to say anything further about puppies, training and Dickens, they hurried out of the door, down the path and out onto the street.

'Bloody hell, Branwell. You took your time!' said Edith as they strode along the pavement.

'I know. His house was like a treasure trove. Just wait until I tell you what I found.'

Ten minutes later, they were back in Edith's flat. Branwell emptied out his pockets and laid the contents on the coffee table.

There were several rolls of undeveloped films in plastic cases and a small pile of photographs.

'He's converted one of the bedrooms into a dark room. There are hundreds of photographs pegged to a drying line and several hundred more pinned to the walls. It's all a little creepy if you ask me. These ones here,' he said, pointing to the black cases, 'I assume he hasn't had a chance to develop yet, so maybe, just maybe, these were taken yesterday?'

Edith picked up one of the film cases and held it between her fingers. 'I didn't realise that Winston was taking pictures too,' she said, setting it back down on the coffee table.

'I suppose it's a natural progression for people like him. A one-time view just isn't enough. They need their images to be immortalised for eternity. It's what gets them off.' He gave an involuntary shudder.

'Yes. But these are hardly pornographic, are they?' said Edith as she began to leaf through the photographs.

They were clandestine images of people going about their daily lives: Felicity Horsfall unlocking the door to her café. Brian Marston collecting the empty glasses from the tables in the pub's beer garden. The most risqué image in the pile was one of Amelia Stokes, the arthritic seventy-year-old who lived two doors down from Winston, collecting in her washing from the line in her dressing gown. There was even one of her and Sarah sitting down on the picnic blanket at the previous week's cricket match, presumably seconds before disaster had struck.

'I thought you'd like that one,' said Branwell, pointing to the photograph. 'It just goes to show that you never know who's watching. Oh, and you'll never guess what was in his bedside cabinet – only a bloody gun!'

'Humm,' said Edith, not paying attention. Her eyes were fixed on the photos as she flicked through them slowly. 'Look how many there are of Felicity. One after the other, after the other. And look at this one! She's standing right outside Harry Lanscombe's front door.'

Branwell snatched the photo from Edith's fingertips and narrowed his eyes. 'Felicity. Wasn't she the one who found the body? Now, that is interesting. So, not only was she first on the murder scene, but we also have evidence that she had contact with the victim prior to his death. Perhaps we should focus our attention on her?' He lowered the photo away from his face. 'Should we tell the detectives what we've found?'

Should they tell the police? Yes. Absolutely, they should. But *were* they going to?

Edith gave a vigorous shake of the head. 'No. We'll just keep this to ourselves for the time being,' and then eyes darted back to Branwell. 'What did you just say about a gun?'

Chapter Twelve

Simon was tucking into his lunch at the station – a rocket and tomato chicken salad that he'd picked up off the shelf in the local supermarket, no less. As portions went, it was pathetic, barely enough to feed a toddler, he thought, as he sulkily forked another mouthful of peppery leaves into his mouth. Emma's comments about going on a diet, coupled with his own realisation that his trousers were that little bit too tight, had forced him to take action. But for the love of god, why hadn't he picked up something with a little more substance rather than this measly plastic tub that weighed lighter than air?

Emma was busy pouring over Harry Lanscombe's bank accounts at her computer, and Simon was just about to

Google the Keto diet when she suddenly called over to him.

'Oh, my word. You have to come and see this,' she said as she stared in amazement at the screen.

Simon, grateful for the break from the bland salad, dropped the fork on his desk and went over to her.

'For somebody who didn't like to part with his cash, he sure as hell had a lot of it,' she said, pointing to the screen.

Simon leaned in closer to the screen, and his eyes widened with surprise. Harry Lanscombe, the village Scrooge, had a balance of just over two hundred thousand pounds in his bank account. Simon let out a long whistle.

'Bloody hell! I'll never understand why the tightest people on the planet are usually loaded,' he said.

'That's why they're rich,' said Emma flatly. 'They barely spend a penny of their own, so it just mounts up in their bank accounts. Wait a minute...look at that deposit there...and again there...and there.'

Simon stared at all of the large cash deposits, five thousand pounds for one. Seven thousand for another. There was even an eye-watering fifteen grand that had been deposited into the account just a few days before Harry was killed.

'We need to find out which branch they were deposited at and see if there's any CCTV. That right there could be our motive.'

'Just like Branwell Allerton told you the other day. Maybe we shouldn't have been so quick to dismiss him,' goaded Emma.

But Simon rolled his eyes. 'Oh, come on, Em. He's old and has nothing better to do than watch crime programmes. He's probably watching CSI as we speak. Now, get on the phone to the bank and see what you can find out.'

He left Emma punching in numbers on the phone and went back to his desk. Finally, they were getting somewhere. He'd originally thought this would be an easy case to solve with there being so many people around, and old people, well, they tended to be so transparent with their lives. But when they'd searched Harry's flat, all they'd discovered was an impeccably clean home with far too many tins of potatoes in the kitchen cupboard. There hadn't been a single clue to suggest that this lonely old man was anything other than a lonely old man.

Simon looked back down at his paltry salad and groaned. He picked it up and threw it in the bin by his feet. Not today, Satan, he thought to himself. He'd start afresh tomorrow instead, as he opened his desk drawer and plucked out his emergency Mars Bar.

Emma slammed down the phone just as he was about to take a bite, and he dropped his hand down into his lap before she could see him.

'Result. It's the village branch, and yes, they do have CCTV. I told them we're on our way to view it,' she said, standing up and sliding her arms in her coat.

Simon opened his desk drawer and dropped the Mars Bar back inside. His whole mouth was salivating, begging for him to bite into the chocolate ooziness, but Simon wasn't about to let Emma see him fail at the first hurdle. He'd pick something up at the village. He might even offer to buy Emma a pub lunch if the bank's cameras turned up trumps.

'Right,' he said, standing and slipping on his own coat. 'Let's go and see what they've got.'

Maybe Simon shouldn't have had high expectations when the bank had said they had CCTV. He'd been expecting high-quality, pixel-perfect images but what they were actually viewing was the very grainy recording of a security system which, like the rest of the village, belonged in the dark ages. He squinted his eyes and moved his head closer to the screen.

'There he is,' said Maureen, the bank clerk. 'I remember him coming in that day because he was all smiles and whistles. Not like Harry at all. Usually, the best you could expect from him was a grunt as he slid over his paying-in slip with a bagful of pennies.'

'So, it was out of character for him to pay in large sums of money?' asked Emma.

Maureen folded her arms and rested them on her large stomach. 'Harry? Large sums of money? Oh yes,' she said, letting out a throaty chuckle. 'Harry Lanscombe very rarely paid in anything over twenty pounds. But over the last couple of months, all of a sudden there he is with a bag brimming with notes. It was like he'd won the lottery or something.'

'Did you ask him where he got it from?' said Simon, and Maureen nodded.

'Of course. The bank has an anti-laundering policy. He said that he won it gambling.'

That old chestnut, thought Simon. 'And did you see anybody with him?'

'No. The poor old soul was always alone.'

'Okay. Well, thanks for that. Would you be able to print off copies of all of the times Mr Lanscombe came into the branch to deposit those sums? We'll need it as evidence.'

Maureen's face broke into a wide grin. 'How exciting! Just wait until I tell my Roger about this. Of course, I'll get those sorted for you. Give me a few minutes.'

Maureen wobbled off into another room.

'I swear to God, this is the most excitement this place has seen in years,' said Emma. 'If I ever get like that, I insist that you shoot me.'

Simon laughed. 'You're a long time away from that yet, Emma. Don't you worry.'

She smiled sweetly back at him. 'Aw, thanks. And I'd do the same for you. Shoot you right between the eyes without hesitation.'

Simon wasn't sure whether to be grateful or downright terrified, but he smiled back at her all the same. 'That's good to know.'

'But obviously, you're a lot closer to that than I am,' she added without a hint of malice.

Chapter Thirteen

E dith and Branwell were sitting in Felicity's little café, unoriginally named Bun in the Oven. She'd left Branwell in charge of the ordering, allowing him the opportunity to work his debonaire magic with Felicity at the counter. Despite his ailing years, there was something captivating about her brother that all women loved. Even when he'd been younger, he'd always portrayed himself as a ladies' man, earning himself a bit of a reputation amongst their father's friends as a serial womaniser at one point, something which had even brought a smile to his permanent sullen face. Branwell was adept at showering women with just the right amount of compliments without making himself appear sleazy. And ultimately, they'd draped themselves over him at the numerous balls they attended or hosted as easily as a coat on a hanger. How disappointing it must have been for them to learn that he wasn't remotely interested in them or their anatomy. To be fair, even Edith had been surprised to learn that her brother was gay. She could understand him wanting to keep it to himself in a time when homosexuality was very much frowned upon – illegal even up until 1967, and although Branwell would have lived through a time of its decriminalisation, the bigoted views were still firmly rooted in society. At least he could be himself now, though, she thought to herself. At least he could be himself around *her*, and that knowledge warmed Edith's heart.

She watched him lean over the counter and whisper something in Felicity's ear, resulting in her bursting into a fit of giggles and giving him a playful slap on the arm.

'You really are a devil,' she giggled at him.

'Good. A devil is much more fun than anything up there,' he said, thumbing towards the ceiling. 'I'd better go and sit down and let you get on with work. But if you get a free five minutes, come and join us.'

He turned and headed back to their table, rolling his eyes at Edith.

'It's all too easy, it really is,' he whispered into her ear. 'I give her five minutes before she's sat with us and playing footsie with me under the table.'

Edith patted the inside of her coat, making sure for the hundredth time that the photos she'd tucked inside the pocket were still there. 'How are we going to approach this?' she asked Branwell.

'Let me at least take a bit of my cake before you jump straight into it,' he replied. 'I've ordered a rainbow slice, whatever that is. I was giving Felicity a bit of a clue, but I think it went straight over her head.'

Edith took a cautious glance around. The café was busy – busier than she'd seen it in a long time. But then her eyes went to the various posters that were sellotaped all over the walls, declaring a forty-percent discount on all orders over ten pounds.

'She must be struggling for business,' said Edith. 'That's quite a generous discount.'

Branwell nodded in agreement. 'You mentioned that she was eager to have the cake stall in the marquee. She'd undercut your friend, Sarah, in order to get it, didn't you say?'

'Yes. So what do you think? What would Felicity be doing at Harry Lanscombe's flat? What would she possibly want from him?'

Branwell held three fingers in the air. 'What did I tell you? Sex. Money. Revenge. They're your three main motives. So, let's look at them individually. Sex?'

They both grimaced and shook their heads in unison. Branwell pushed down one finger.

'Okay. That leaves money and revenge,' continued Branwell. 'So, money. Given what we think about this place, do we think she was after that from Harry? Maybe she borrowed money from him, and she snuffed him out so that she didn't have to pay him back? And then there's revenge. What could she be revengeful over?'

A thought dropped into Edith's brain, and she snapped her fingers together. 'Perhaps Harry did to Felicity what he did to everybody else? You know, complained about the service or the food. Maybe he threatened to report Felicity to Environmental Health like he did with Lorraine at the Shop & Save?'

'Well, there's only one way to find out,' said Branwell, lowering his hand back down and smiling sweetly as Felicity sashayed over with a heaving tray expertly balanced on one hand.

'And there we are. One Death by chocolate slice for you, Edith,' she said, placing a stomach-busting slice of cake in front of her. 'And one of my special rainbow slices for you, Branwell,' she added, setting down an equally large, if not larger, slice of cake in front of her brother. 'And two coffees. Oh, and not forgetting my own drink,' she finished, putting a cup in front of her.

She pulled out the chair next to Branwell, sat down and then shuffled it dangerously close to him. Edith suppressed her smile. Any closer, and she'd be sitting on his lap.

'You seem quite busy lately,' said Edith, gesturing around the café with her fork. 'Things must be going well for you.'

Felicity gave a non-committal nod but said nothing as she picked up her coffee cup and sipped politely.

'But then again, the large discount has probably helped bring in business,' added Branwell casually. 'Although I would have thought that you wouldn't have needed it. Not with these beauties that you sell.' He pointed down at the monstrous wedge of cake in front of him.

Edith used her fork to cut a small corner off the edge of the cake and slipped it into her mouth. Shop brought. She'd eaten enough cakes over the years to know the difference.

'Have the police questioned you again about Harry?' she asked Felicity.

Felicity rolled her eyes and set her cup back down on the table. 'Good Lord, yes. It's been relentless. Question after question. And it's the same thing they're asking. Did I see Harry in the days leading up to his murder? Did I have any contact with him on the day of the cricket match? Did Harry ever come into the café? Did he complain about anything here so he could get a discount? On and on and on.'

'And did you?' asked Branwell. 'Have any contact with Harry, I mean? Were you and he...' He let the words linger.

Felicity pulled a horrified expression. 'What? Me and Harry? I may have been single for a while, but I haven't lowered my standards quite that low, I assure you.'

'But you did have some dealings with him, though, didn't you?' added Edith, thinking of the photograph of Felicity's smiling face as she stood on Harry's doorstep.

'No. I had no contact with that man whatsoever,' the woman replied curtly. The old-fashioned bell above the door to the café tinkled, heralding the entrance of a customer, and Felicity scraped back her chair and stood abruptly.

'Listen, thanks for the chat, but I really should be getting on. I don't like to keep my customers waiting,' she told them as she moved to head back to the counter.

'Just one more thing, Felicity,' said Edith. 'Did Harry ever come in here and make any complaints?'

She shot Edith a puzzled look. 'Complaints about here? No. He came in quite a few times – each time, he ordered the same thing: a latte with a slice of lemon drizzle cake.'

'And not once did he try to get a discount?' said Branwell. 'But that was Harry's MO. He was famous for it in the village.'

Felicity's face darkened, and she moved closer to the table. 'I can categorically tell you that Harry never,' she whispered at them both, 'came here and complained about my business. He always ordered the same thing. And he always paid in full. He even left a tip! Now, if that's all, I really have to get on.'

Felicity returned to the counter, flushed and flustered, as she took the customer's order.

'What do you make of that?' said Branwell. He picked up his cake and took a giant mouthful. 'Truth or fiction?'

What *did* Edith make of that? Something just didn't fit.

She opened her napkin, placed the cake inside and folded the sides around the edges to make a little parcel. She'd keep that for later, she thought to herself as she slid it inside her handbag.

'Well, we know she's lying about seeing Harry before he died. But I believe her when she says that Harry never tried to get a discount here. Which begs the question, why? Why, when Harry was notorious for it, did he come here and pay...' she looked over at the price list on the board on the wall behind Felicity's head and did a mental calculation, 'almost nine pounds for a slice of cake and a drink. Him. Harry. The man who never paid full price for anything. It's all a little odd.'

Branwell placed his elbow on the table and held up two fingers. 'So, if you're right and Harry never said a bad word about this place, then I guess we can rule revenge out,' he said, lowering one of his fingers. 'Which only leaves money.'

Edith ignored the fact that her brother was holding up his middle finger to her, something which he'd done deliberately, judging from the large grin on his face. But Branwell was right. If Harry's murder wasn't about sex or revenge, as far as Felicity was concerned, then the only logical motive remaining was indeed money. And considering that money seemed to play such a prominent role in Harry's life then it was most certainly a possibility.

'I think we need to find out more about Harry's finances,' she said to Branwell. 'And we should also get these films developed. If we hurry, we should be able to make it before the shop closes.

Chapter Fourteen

Emma was sitting in the car, tapping her hands rhythmically against the steering wheel to the beat of the latest Justin Bieber song as she waited for Simon to come out of the village newsagents. He'd told her that he was only going to pick up a copy of the Racing Post, but Emma knew for a fact that Simon detested horse racing, and the fact that she spotted him shovelling a KitKat chunky down his neck through the window, told her all she needed to know. She wasn't a detective for nothing, you know.

Let him get on with it, she thought to herself. It wasn't her body that was getting ruined by the sugary overload. When were people going to understand that, as a species, they weren't designed to eat crap like that? That the modern Western diet of processed, salty and fatty foods was slowly poisoning their bodies. It didn't take a genius to work out the connection between the increase in obesity and chronic illnesses. No. Emma was a total convert to natural foods. She only ate meat and vegetables – unless she was drunk on a night out with friends, where she'd occasionally demolish a doner kebab: She wasn't a nun, for Christ's sake.

As she sat there, shaking her head in dismay at Simon's secret KitKat munching, she happened to turn her head and glance over at Felicity Horsfall's café on the other side of the road.

They'd repeatedly questioned her about her relationship with Harry Lanscombe. Something didn't quite stack up there, as far as Emma was concerned, and she'd adopted the bad cop routine to ram that fact home to Felicity. She was definitely hiding something, but what that something was had so far eluded her. Emma had a knack for these things.

She watched Felicity amble over to one of the tables with a provocative sway of her hips, leaning over more than was necessary to no doubt expose her cleavage just a little to whoever was sitting at the table. Emma knew all the tricks. She'd used them often enough on her Tinder dates.

But she had been surprised to see Edith Elliott and her brother Branwell at the table Felicity was waiting on. If Felicity was flirting with Branwell, then she was wasting her time. The man was clearly gay, in Emma's opinion, although Simon completely disagreed with her on that score. They'd had a heated debate about it over lunch the day before.

She continued watching as Felicity sat down and moved her chair closer to Branwell. It all seemed quite amiable at first. But then suddenly, the atmosphere changed, and Emma spotted the tension in Felicity's back after Edith said something.

If she didn't know better, she'd swear that Edith and Branwell were questioning her. Emma had grown accustomed to body language. She'd interviewed enough suspects over the years to spot it: The clench of a jaw muscle, the twitch in the corner of the mouth, and a little squint of the eye always let her know whether or not she was on the right track.

Felicity had suddenly stood to her feet, and Emma could tell that the woman was a breath away from flinging the chair across the room. Whatever had been said at that table had clearly riled her. She'd scurried away back to the safety of behind the counter to take an order, and Emma's eyes went back to Edith and Branwell, who'd huddled together across the table, whispering something to each other as their eyes went back over to Felicity.

Oh God. Armchair detectives. Just what they needed, thought Emma. There was one in every case lately, it seemed. It wasn't that she was adverse to people offering their help. If they had a juicy piece of information that could move the case forward, then it was welcome. But it was the people who took it upon themselves to get involved privately to try and solve the case on their own. Didn't Edith and Branwell realise that they were hunting a murderer? If they've killed once, then there was nothing to suggest that they wouldn't do it again if they felt threatened.

She'd have to have a word with Simon about it and see what he thought. Perhaps, he could go around to Edith's flat and tell her, in no uncertain terms, to back off and leave it with them – the professionals who had a wealth of resources available to them.

Simon, suitably sugared up, returned to the car and dropped into the driver's seat with a smile.

'All good?' asked Emma, eying up his mouth for any tell-tale remnants of chocolate she could point out to him.

'Grand,' replied Simon.

'Where's the Racing Post? I thought that's what you went in there for?' she said.

Simon's eyes widened at the realisation he'd forgotten to pick up a copy. 'Oh,' they didn't have any left,' he blustered.

Emma raised an unconvinced eyebrow. 'Whatever you say,' she replied slyly.

At that moment, Edith and Branwell exited the café and trotted off down the road.

'We need to have a word about Tweedledee and Tweedledum over there,' she said, pointing over at them.

'Oh? What about?'

'I'll tell you as you drive,' she told him. 'Where are we off to next?'

Simon turned the key in the ignition, and the engine hummed to life. 'Back to the station. I want to dig a little deeper into Harry Lanscombe's history. There must be some family out there.'

He put the car into gear, released the handbrake and sped off down the road, straight past an oblivious Edith and Branwell.

Chapter Fifteen

Winston searched the dark room again. He'd looked under the table, the cluttered window sill, behind the door and the pockets of the lab coat he wore when he was developing the film; well, he had to look the part, didn't he? But his search had yielded zero results.

He stood in the middle of the room, scratching his head and glancing around the floor as though the rolls would magically reappear.

'What have I done with the blasted things?'

Winston went back down the stairs and carried systematic reconstruction of his movements from the second he'd got back in the house after the cricket match the other day. He mimed taking off his coat and hooking it on the peg by the front door. He then knelt down by Dickens, also imaginary, as his dog was currently lying under the living room window fast asleep. He then plodded into the kitchen, filled the kettle with water and flicked down the switch. And then plodded heavy footsteps out of the kitchen, back up the stairs and pretended to empty his trouser pockets and place the invisible contents on the side next to the tray of developing fluid. It was the same process for him each and every time he came back from his excursions. And yet, the four rolls of film were nowhere to be seen.

The only deviation in his movements had been not to develop them straight away after he'd had his first cup of tea. He'd held off doing that on that particular day, given the untimely death of Harry Lanscombe. But Winston didn't need a photograph to show him who had tiptoed around the back of the marquee that afternoon. He'd seen them as clear as day through the end of the lens of the camera as he'd clicked away.

Initially, he hadn't thought too much about it. As the rain set in and the spectators had filled the marquee, Harry had emerged a few minutes later, and looked over at the long queue for the toilets with dismay. Winston had stayed rooted in his secret spot, twisting the end of the lens this way and that to adjust the focus for a clearer picture, when Harry took a cautious glance around himself and then proceeded to disappear behind the marquee, no doubt preferring to take a wee at the back of the tent rather than join the ridiculous queue.

And then he'd seen them. Anybody else viewing might have thought it odd that that person was sneaking behind the marquee after Harry. But not Winston. He'd seen them with him several times before, at Harry's house and the other person's house. He knew there was something untoward going on, but he just didn't know what. Harry and the other person were just two people he would have never put together, and he'd always found it strange how they refused to even acknowledge each other when other people were around. It was most definitely fishy business going on between them, but Winston had no interest in discovering exactly what it was. All he was interested in was his little hobby. It wasn't about the finer details, just the visuals that kept him entertained.

He'd got a good shot of them emerging and scanning the area around them too. And then seconds later, the scream went up, and the whole of the village seemed to descend. He'd got some brilliant action shots that day; ones which might have come in rather useful at a later date. He should have bloody developed them immediately, just as would any other time, but his thoughts had been conflicted over it all.

He didn't want to believe that they could have done something like that – he wouldn't believe it. Winston had always found them to be such a lovely person. How could it be possible that they were suddenly caving a man's head in? The pieces of the jigsaw refused to slot together in his mind. Harry must have done something, said something, to inflame the situation. That's it, decided Winston. This must be Harry's fault because that was the only thing that made sense to him.

And if it had been Harry's fault, then there was no way that Winston was going to give those films to the police. He, Winston Mayhew, had somebody else's life in his hands. He had the power to hand it back to them or destroy it completely, and the responsibility had weighed heavily on his mind for days. But not now. Now, he knew exactly what he was going to do. He was going to destroy the films and let the whole thing blow over. And he'd have a discreet word with them too, you know, for moral support. He'd make it clear that he knew what they'd done to Harry, and if they wanted to tell Winston why, then all the better. They do say that a problem shared is a problem halved, after all.

But all that was slightly scuppered now that the films had gone missing. Yes, now that he thought about it, he definitely took them straight upstairs to the developing room. He distinctly remembered being so excited by what had happened that he hadn't even stopped to put the kettle on. But if that was the case, then where the hell had they disappeared to?

'Coat off. Upstairs. On the side. Coat off. Upstairs. On the side,' he repeated over and over to himself.

Had he gone to the toilet before entering the spare room? No. Definitely not. He'd gone straight into the dark room.

He let out a frustrated sigh and then growled loudly. A few moments later, Dickens's soft paws padded up the stairs and into the dark room to see what all the fuss was about. He lay down at Winston's feet and exposed his belly, ready for the rubs to commence. Winston let out a throaty chuckle and knelt down next to his dog to oblige to his animal's whims.

'You are such a good boy,' he said. 'Such a good...' Winston suddenly stopped stroking Dickens and stood up straight.

A memory of Edith's brother, Branwell, fussing Dickens jumped across Winston's synapses.

Branwell had left the room to use the toilet – he'd been an extraordinary length of time, too. Winston had assumed that he had some kind of bowl problem at first, but come to think of it, when he'd gone upstairs with a bottle of bleach and a candle after they'd left, there'd be no foul smell lingering. He hadn't thought much about it then and had duly given the toilet bowl a good squirt of bleach anyway, seeing as he was already up there.

Had Branwell been mooching around his rooms? It seemed the only logical answer given the circumstances. Winston's face darkened at the thought of somebody poking about in his business where he had no right to be and his inner Sergeant Major resurfaced as he formulated his plan of action.

Firstly, he'd call round at Edith's flat and see if that kleptomaniac brother of hers was there and retrieve his films. And then he'd call round at Harry's unfortunate murderer's house and reassure them that as far as he was concerned they had absolutely nothing to worry about. Their secret was safe with him. They could trust him.

Winston would never blab or give the game away. He'd never even mention it again.

He'd make sure that he took it to the grave with him.

Chapter Sixteen

The last customer had finally left the café, and Felicity hurriedly locked the door behind them, flipped over the placard declaring the shop closed, pressed her back against the door and let out a sigh. Thank God today was over with.

Initially, when she'd first opened up that morning, she'd been absolutely fine. Sure, the interviews with the police had been tough and had weighed heavily on her mind. She'd been terrified every time the phone rang, convinced that they were going to ask her to go down to the station again. Or each time the bell sounded at the café door, she'd been too frightened to look just in case it was DCI Jackman and the super-svelte DS Emma Hooper standing in the doorway, notebooks poised at the ready so that they could start interrogating her again.

But her fears had been allayed with each hour that had progressed, and just when Felicity felt as though she was able to breathe normally again, her anxiety had peaked back up to dangerous levels when Edith Elliott and that bloody brother of hers had started to quiz her all over again.

Who did they think they were? The bloody Gestapo? The cheek of them, coming into her little shop, eating her cakes, well, the cakes were courtesy of the wholesalers, but nobody needed to know that, and then they'd proceeded to bombard her with questions. She'd seen the way they'd looked at her as they scrutinised her responses.

It wouldn't have been half as bad if Felicity hadn't been lying, but unfortunately for her, she'd been holding back a whole sorry tale, fearful that if anybody found out, they might think that it'd been her who'd killed Harry Lanscombe.

'That bloody man!' she shouted with frustration. 'That bloody, horrible, cruel man.'

She burst into tears and hurried over to one of the tables to retrieve a paper napkin. She dabbed her eyes, but the tears refused to stop, and she was soon blubbing and snorting uncontrollably.

She should have never got involved with Harry. Technically, it had been all her fault. She'd been the one to go along with it all. It wasn't like anybody held a gun to her head and made her do it. She believed what Harry had told her; trusted him completely. And then poof. Within the space of a couple of weeks, her whole life had been turned upside down and utterly destroyed.

Felicity should have trusted her gut. Her mother had always told her that you should never ignore your instincts. But no. Felicity had been spun a line, and she'd fallen for it, hook, line and sinker. When something seemed too good to be true, it usually was – another one of her mother's favourite, if not repetitive, sayings.

'Oh bugger off, Mother,' she shouted out, even though the old lady had been dead for eight years.

What was she going to do? What the hell *could* she do? She was knee-deep in a whole shower of dog mess, and at that moment, she had no idea how to wade herself out of it.

Harry Lanscombe, the lovely rogue: The man who had always liked to save a penny or two here and there had, in his own magical way, ruined her life.

She should tell the police everything, regardless of the outcome. That was the only thing that would save her now. If she continued lying for much longer, they would stop believing her altogether.

Lying. Lied. Liar.

She, Felicity Horsfall, was a liar.

She'd lied to the police, and now everything was about to come crashing down around her. They wouldn't believe her—not now.

Felicity grasped at her chest as her heart beat furiously against her ribcage. She needed to speak to somebody, somebody who wasn't going to judge her and who could tell her that she had nothing to be frightened of. Somebody who told her that everything was going to be okay and to stop worrying herself.

She needed to explain everything to somebody. She needed that vent—that outlet—to release some of the pressure bubbling under the surface of her skin. If she didn't talk to somebody soon, she'd explode. She was never much good when it came to bad situations. But this was more than just a bad situation. It was a hopeless situation, and Felicity cursed the day she'd ever met Harry Lanscombe and listened to his stupid ideas.

She flicked off the lights, reached for her handbag and coat and rushed out of the front door in search of support. But from whom, she had no idea.

Chapter Seventeen

Edith handed the plastic tubs of camera film across the desk.

'How quickly can you get these developed?' she asked.

The young, spotty teenager picked up one of the tubs and stared at it in wonderment.

'Wow! I've heard about these things, but I've never seen one before,' he said.

Branwell sidled up next to Edith and laughed. 'It's a roll of film, not a Fabergé egg.'

The teenager lowered the tub back down and looked curiously at Branwell. 'A faber-what?'

'Never mind that,' interrupted Edith before her brother started giving the poor boy a lesson on antiques. 'How long would it take to get them developed?'

The boy gave a bored huff and reached underneath the counter. He pulled out a card and scanned the details.

'It'll be about a week, according to this. A week? God, that's insane. Most people take pictures on their phones nowadays. You can get them printed off immediately when you connect your phone by Bluetooth to the printer over there,' he pointed to a small machine in the corner of the shop. 'There's just not much demand for old-fashioned printing anymore.'

'Noted,' said Branwell. 'But is a week really the best you can do? Surely, there's an express service?'

The boy sighed and reluctantly checked the card again. 'Oh,' he said with surprise. 'You're right You can get them back in three days. But it'll cost an extra £9.99. Is that cool with you?'

Edith nodded. 'Very cool. Let's go with that one, shall we?'

They emerged from the shop ten minutes later. Edith tucked the receipt deep into her handbag, and they made the short journey back to her flat.

'I must say,' said Branwell. 'All of this walking has been wonderful. It's saved me a fortune in fuel for the Bentley. And I'm pretty sure that a new muscle has formed in my legs. Here – feel it,' he said as he stretched out one of his legs and tensed.

'I think I'll pass, thank you,' said Edith, smiling. 'Put your leg down before one of the old dears sees you and passes out.'

He gave her a playful nudge in her side. 'I hate to break it to you, but you're one of those old dears now. In fact, we're both old dears. Who'd have thought, eh?'

They walked arm in arm under the warm April sunshine in silence. As villages went, she'd always thought hers to be idyllic. Very few houses ever came up for sale in Hinklebury owing to the fact that when somebody moved in, they rarely moved out again. Everybody seemed to know each other, and there wasn't a day that went past when Edith walked down the street and somebody called out hello to her. If somebody was ill, then there were always kindly neighbours to look after them. When somebody's car broke down, there was an offer of a lift. She loved it here. But there had always been something missing for her. She hadn't noticed it at first, not when the children and Ronnie were there. But when Alex and Charlotte moved away from the area, she felt a ping of regret deep in her heart. And then, when Ronnie passed away, the feeling deepened. All of a sudden, Edith had been left alone with nothing but her thoughts. It had been inevitable that they'd often drifted back to her family and her days at Althorp Hall, mainly her mother and Branwell – her father could rot in hell for all she cared. She'd dreamt about being reunited with Branwell, about seeking him out, and she'd often found herself in floods of tears whenever she'd watched *Long Lost Family* on television. In a way, she never imagined that she herself would be playing her own part in her own episode, where Branwell would once again be at her side, saying stupid things and making her smile. How she'd missed him. And now, here he was again; it was as though they'd never been apart, as though those fifty years had been no more than the blink of an eye.

'Edith,' said Branwell, breaking the silence. 'I need to talk to you about something.'

'Oh?' she said. 'What's that?'

Branwell opened his mouth to speak but then closed it again when Sarah Winslow came into view, standing outside Edith's flat.

'I'll tell you later,' he replied as they neared the woman.

Sarah, spotting them, gave them a generous smile and wiggled a cake tin in the air.

'I felt a little hemmed in at mine, so I thought I'd pop over. Anyone for cake?'

Edith's mind went to the huge piece of cake from the café she still had tucked away in her handbag, but she smiled back at her friend and nodded.

'What a lovely idea. Come on, let's get inside and get that kettle on.'

'Have the police come to see you again?' asked Sarah. She took a huge bite out of her carrot cake and gave a groan of appreciation. 'Umm. Delicious.'

Edith shook her head. 'No. They haven't been to see me. What did they ask you?'

Sarah flicked cake crumbs off her lap and onto Edith's carpet. 'They just went over the same things as the other day. It's a waste of manpower if you ask me. No wonder they moan that they haven't got enough money when they waste so much of their time repeating themselves.'

'I suppose you could say that they were being extra vigilant,' offered Branwell. He held up his empty plate to Sarah, who beamed back at him and duly plonked another slice of cake on his plate.

'Yes. I suppose you're right, Branwell,' she told him. 'And it's funny how sometimes they manage to pluck out information that you didn't even realise was there. Something so inconsequential that we mere mortals can't see it. It must be something they're trained for. Do you think?'

Edith tilted her head. 'What information is that? Did you see something?'

Sarah nodded eagerly. 'I didn't think too much of it at the time. But the more they quizzed me, it was like a door opened in my memory, and out it popped.'

'Out what popped?' asked Branwell.

Sarah lowered her plate to the coffee table. 'It was about a week ago, you see. I'd just come back from visiting you, Edith, in the hospital. Maybe that's why I'd forgotten all about it? Because I had other things on my mind. Anyway, they asked me to recount my movements, where I'd been, who I'd spoken to and all that, and that's when I remembered.'

'Remembered what exactly?' said Edith, who was perilously close to planting Sarah's face straight into her cake if she didn't hurry up.

Sarah clapped her hands together gleefully, like a happy toddler. 'I remembered that I'd seen Harry Lanscombe's son standing outside his front door. He was banging on the door, and at one point, he bent down and shouted something through the letterbox.'

'Harry's got a son? I didn't know that,' said Edith. 'How did you know it was his son?'

Sarah chuckled. 'He's easy to spot. He's over six foot tall, covered in tattoos and has a bright purple mohawk on his head.'

Branwell sat up in the chair. 'Over six feet tall with tattoos? That's just how I like my men,' he said, winking at Edith.

'And what happened after he shouted through the letterbox?' continued Edith, ignoring him.

Sarah shrugged her shoulders. 'I couldn't tell you. I carried on home. But it did seem to please the detectives when I told them. They were practically rubbing their hands together with glee. I think they were in a bit of a lull, suspect-wise.'

So, Harry had a son. A secret son? Or estranged? Clearly, it was one or the other because, in all her years of living in the village, she had never seen nor heard Harry mention that he had a grown child. Could it be that there was a long-running feud between them? Certainly, if Sarah had seen him shouting at his father through his letterbox, it indicated that something wasn't quite right between them both. If only she could find out more about this man and have the opportunity to speak to him it would make things become more clearer. She needed to find out who this man was, but how? Maybe if she went to the police and handed over the photographs of Felicity outside Harry's home, they'd be inclined to tell her. That was it – she and Branwell would go to the police station in the morning and ask to see DCI Jackman and DS Hooper and see if they were interested in a favour for a favour.

'I have to say,' said Sarah. 'That was the most delicious cake I've ever eaten, even if I do say so myself.' She rose to her feet, replaced the lid on the half-filled cake tin and tucked it underneath her arm. 'But I really should be going now. There's a documentary about the mating rituals of Orangutans that I really can't miss. Will I see you tomorrow?' she added, looking hopefully over at Edith.

Edith nodded back at her. 'Branwell and I are busy in the morning, but I'm sure we can meet later in the afternoon if you're free.'

She showed Sarah to the door, waved her off for the short journey home, and then returned to the living room.

Branwell looked up at her as she entered, rubbing his cake-filled stomach. 'Sister mine,' he said to her. 'If I ever tell you that I have to be home so that I can catch the documentary on the mating rituals of the Orangutan, then I want you to promise me that you'll immediately beat me to death with a rolling pin.'

Edith smiled. 'Deal,' she replied without hesitating.

Chapter Eighteen

Winston pulled back the net curtains in his living room and took another look at the deserted pavements. Where were they? He'd specifically told them to be there by half past seven. He wanted this whole thing done and dusted by eight so that he still had time to go out for his evening walk with Dickens – and his trusty binoculars, of course. Most of the villagers tended to close their curtains by nine o'clock, and Winston had quickly discovered that there was nothing worth seeing at all past quarter past nine. He'd give them five more minutes, but after that, that was it.

They'd seemed so surprised when Winston had first nervously approached them and told them what he knew. Through many coughs and splutters, he'd stated, as softly as an ex-military man could, that he knew that they'd killed Harry Lanscombe, and although he didn't know why they'd done it, he was sure that they'd had a damn good reason to do so.

The man had been a nuisance, a blight on the village, and over the years, he'd managed to secure himself as enemy number one with many of the residents, so all things considered, they'd probably done everybody a massive favour.

Winston had neglected to tell them that he had evidence, or more accurately, Edith and her nosey brother had the evidence that, if it fell into the police's hands, they'd find themselves behind bars faster than you could say 'you're nicked'. He didn't see the point of it, seeing as he was never going to use it against them. And there was little point saying anything until the undeveloped film was safely back in his hands anyway.

All Winston wanted to know was *why* they'd done it. As far as he could tell, they had no association with Harry Lanscombe, directly or indirectly, and there was the small part of him that needed to know the intricate details in order for his regimented mind to make sense of it all.

He was well-versed in the art of war and knew that sometimes conflicts, although he might not have personally agreed with the politics surrounding them, were necessary. On several occasions, he'd had to put his beliefs aside, slap on his warpaint, and go out onto the field in the name of righteousness. And as with any war, there were always casualties.

When the shock of Winston's knowledge had died down, they'd thanked him profusely for his kindness and understanding and by the end of the brief conversation, they'd promised to come to his home and tell him exactly what had led to Harry's death. They'd insisted that they hadn't wanted to do it, but Harry, as Winston could well believe, had backed them into a corner and left them with no other choice.

Up until that day, Winston had had very little to do with them. He said hello and goodbye to them whenever he'd seen them in the street, but other than that, their connection had been nothing more than a cordial one. But now Winston felt a little flutter of excitement in his stomach swirl as he realised that in the five minutes they'd been talking, they'd built a real connection with each other. Maybe Winston was on the verge of having his first proper friend?

As he stood there waiting, one eye on the mantlepiece clock as the minutes ticked by, he wondered whether today and all the days that followed would be filled with the company of somebody else other than just Dickens. It would be nice to have a conversation and, for once, for somebody to respond to him and offer their opinions rather than making do with the occasional woof from the dog or the usual crippling silence. Yes. He was looking forward to having a companion in his life – a human companion. What a refreshing change it was going to be.

Suddenly, his life had taken on a new meaning. One of possibilities, and fun and friendship. Just look at how much Edith had changed now that her brother had come back into her life. She'd always been so aloof before, more so after that wretched husband of hers had passed away. Winston had despised that man; he had been a cruel and controlling drunk, and he'd expected Edith to have flourished into life after he'd died, but instead, she'd shrank back into her little shell with nobody there to help pull her out again. Winston had offered his services, obviously. He'd knocked on her door more times than he cared to remember with little Tupperware pots of casseroles and asking if she'd like to join him on a walk or two with Dickens. He thought for one mistaken moment that he and Edith might have grown closer because of their shared grief, but she'd shunned him away without even trying.

Well, Mrs Elliott. That was fine by him. She'd actually done him a favour by declining his affections because if she hadn't, he'd have been shackled to her and not able to enjoy the fun that was potentially coming for him.

The doorbell let out a satisfying ring, and Winston, immersed in his thoughts, jumped. Finally! He straightened his shirt, ran a hand through his wispy, balding hair, and checked that the zip on his trousers was up, and then hurried to answer the door.

'Yes,' he said to his dog, who hadn't even flinched from his slumber at the sound of the doorbell. 'Today is going to be the day that our luck is changing, dear boy. You mark my words.'

Chapter Nineteen

Simon placed his elbows on the table in the interview room, closed his eyes and, in a circular motion, rubbed his temples with his index fingers.

'So, let me get this straight. You're saying that you've been withholding potential evidence which could potentially solve an active murder case?'

He let his arms drop heavily onto the table and glared at the two people sitting on the other side, seemingly unconcerned at his obvious annoyance.

'You used the word potentially too many times in that sentence,' offered Branwell. 'I would have just applied it once.'

'Thanks for your insight there, Wordsworth,' Simon snapped back. 'Now, back to what I was saying – the evidence. Can I ask what it is?'

'Yes,' said Edith.

Silence loomed in the air in the interview room.

'Well, do you think you could expand on that and tell us what it is?' he said with a tinge of frustration.

Edith looked at Branwell. Branwell looked over at Simon and then to Emma before looking back at Edith and shrugging his shoulders.

'Of for the love of God!' bellowed Emma. 'Will you or won't you tell us what the evidence is?' She slapped the palm of her hand down heavily on the thick case file she'd brought in with her.

'That all depends on whether or not you're prepared to help me with something,' said Edith. 'I may, and I stress the word may...'

'In which she means, she does,' interrupted Branwell.

'Require a certain piece of information from you,' she finished.

Emma slowly turned her head to Simon, who was sitting staring back at the pensioners in total disbelief. She motioned her head towards the door and stood up. Without uttering another word, Simon rose from his chair and followed her outside the room.

'We should do them for withholding evidence and be done with it,' she whispered to him. 'I warned you, didn't I? I told you they fancied themselves as detectives. That's the problem with these oldies sometimes; they've got nothing better to do with their time '

Simon held out his palm, trying to diffuse her irritation. 'I hear you. And yes, it appears that you were right. But before go back in there, all guns blazing, arresting two ageing members of the community, and finding ourselves being slapped with a police intimidation complaint, let me try one more time to get through to them. Sometimes, the softly softly approach is far more effective.'

She nodded her agreement back at him, took a deep breath, and they headed back inside.

'Right. Mrs Elliott. Mr Allerton. I've consulted with my sergeant, and we've decided that at this present time, we're going to have to politely decline your request for information. Unless, of course, that request has absolutely nothing to do with the investigation. Does it?'

Edith shook her head. 'No. It has everything to do with the investigation,' she told him.

'Well, in that case, it's a firm no from us,' continued Simon. 'So, I'm going to ask you again to hand over the information that you have and allow us to be the judge of its relevance to the investigation. Otherwise, we might be inclined to proceed with a legal route to obtain it.'

Simon sat back in his chair, pleased with his diplomatic speech. Sometimes, members of the public just needed reminding who was actually in charge.

Branwell gave Edith a nudge in the ribs and gave her an all-knowing nod of the head.

'Of course, Detective,' replied Edith. She reached into her handbag and pulled out a small wad of photographs and slid them across the table.

Simon picked them up and began to leaf through the photos. 'Where did you get these?' he asked, passing over one that showed Felicity standing outside Harry Lanscombe's property.

Emma took the photo from his hands, and her eyes widened.

'Winston Mayhew,' said Edith. 'I did tell you, didn't I, that he liked to watch people. Granted, I didn't know that he was also taking photographs, but there you have it.'

'And Mr Mayhew just handed these over to you, did he?' asked Emma, her brows narrowing with suspicion.

'Strictly speaking, no,' Branwell said bluntly. 'We just happened to be visiting Mr Mayhew, and all of a sudden, I found myself needing to use the loo. And when I went upstairs, I got a little lost and found myself in a makeshift dark room that he'd set up in one of the bedrooms. Obviously, I was about to walk straight back out again, but I saw a few photographs just lying on the table, so I thought I'd just take a little look. I've no idea how they ended up in my pocket. I didn't realise until Edith and I had returned home. We were on the verge of taking them straight back when I discovered them, but upon closer inspection, we thought that they might be important, so we thought it best to bring them here.'

'How very public-spirited of you,' said Emma as she passed the photograph back to Simon. ' And I can totally see how you might get lost in the upstairs of a three-bedroom semi. It happens to me all the time.'

Edith snapped the clasp on her handbag closed and then got up from the chair. 'Well, if that's all, detectives, we should leave you to get on with your work. I'm sure that you're extremely busy.'

Branwell got up too and rushed to the door before his sister. He opened the door, allowing Edith to go ahead before him, and then he turned back to face Simon and Emma. 'Good day to you, detectives,' he said, doffing an imaginary hat. And with that, they were gone.

'I've decided,' began Emma, shifting in her chair to face Simon. 'I hate people. I think I should resign.'

Simon smiled. 'While I agree that you're not exactly a people person, you are an excellent detective. So, before you go, can we at least close this case? It seems that Mr Mayhew and Ms Horsfall have certainly got a lot of explaining to do.'

'Agreed,' replied Emma. 'Let's go and see Mr Peeping Tom first. I bloody knew he was lying to us the other day.'

She stood up and stretched her arms above her head, yawning loudly, and her top lifted slightly, exposing her tiny midriff. That girl needed to eat more burgers, thought Simon. He subconsciously pulled his own stomach in, thinking back to the full English fry-up he'd devoured that morning before coming to the police station: two sausages, two pieces of bacon, a fried egg, mushrooms cooked in butter, tomatoes, baked beans, black pudding, and a slice of fried bread. It had been absolutely delicious – should see him through until dinner time, he told himself. But his stomach let out a loud grumble as though reminding Simon he was fooling nobody but himself.

They drove straight to Winston Mayhew's house, and throughout the whole journey, Emma had been lecturing Simon on the perils of fatty foods, even referring to the full English breakfasts on several occasions. Simon had causally inspected his mouth in the rear-view mirror to check that he hadn't got half a mushroom wedged in between his teeth somewhere. In the end, after the third specific comment about healthy breakfasts, he looked over at her and asked her outright.

'How did you know?'

Emma popped the lid back onto her lipstick and dropped it back into her bag. 'I saw your car parked outside the Silly Sausage on my way to work. It didn't need a genius to put two and two together.'

'It's like having my own personal bodyguard working with you,' he said drily, annoyed that Emma had somehow, yet again, caught him out.

'Not at all,' she replied. 'A bodyguard's job is to protect. You're past help, I'm afraid.'

'Oh, cheers,' he shot back.

That was the problem with Emma; she was unintentionally honest but in the most brutal way. She never intended to say things which caused offence, but somewhere between thinking something and the words spilling off her tongue, her remarks always seemed to land like a punch to the guts. That was the reason she was single, in Simon's opinion; she was far too harsh with her boyfriends. She'd once told one that the reason she refused to kiss him was because his breath smelled permanently of onions, even though he never ate the damn things. He'd ghosted her phone calls and messages soon after that. And there was another time when after just two dates, she told him that his job in a call centre was just a cover for laziness and lack of ambition as casually as if she'd been asking what he wanted for dinner that evening.

Simon had tried and failed on several occasions to get her to soften up. Maybe there was some deep-rooted childhood trauma somewhere in her history that could explain her behaviour. But Emma, ever the professional, had poo-poohed his idea as sentimental hogwash and told him in no uncertain terms that she was the way she was and there was nothing she wanted to change. Oh well, each to their own.

They parked the car outside Winston's house, got out and headed up the little path to the front door. Seasonal bulbs neatly lined the slabs, displaying bursts of rainbow colours like a cheery welcome.

'Sir,' said Emma quietly as she pointed to the front door.

Simon looked up and noted the open door. It didn't appear to have been forced, but even so, not many people left the doors wide open these days, even in a picturesque village such as this. He crept in front of Emma, pushing her protectively behind him, and stepped inside.

'Mr Mayhew,' he called out. 'It's the police.'

Simon strained his ears, but all that greeted them was the unmistakable whine of Dickens coming from behind the kitchen door. He opened the door to the kitchen, and the dog bounded into the hallway, wagging his tail gratefully.

'Hello, you,' said Simon, patting the dog on the head. 'Where's your owner, eh?'

He moved further along the hallway to the closed living room door. He looked back at Emma, her phone poised in her hand, ready to call the station if the need arose. He nodded at her. She nodded back, and Simon pushed down the handle and slowly opened the door.

Winston Mayhew was sitting in the armchair, his back to the door.

'Mr Mayhew?' Simon asked again as he cautiously entered the room. 'Are you okay?'

He went around to the front of the chair and stood up straight. 'You'd better call it in,' he told Emma. 'Somebody's shot him. He's dead.'

Chapter Twenty

E dith and Branwell were sitting in Edith's flat, staring at the scrap of paper that Branwell had used to hastily scribble down the details of Harry Lanscombe's son.

'It was their own fault for leaving the file on the desk,' said Branwell. 'Nobody could blame us for taking a peek. And anyway, you handed the photographs over to them, so no harm done.'

When DCI Jackman and DS Hooper had left them alone in the interview room, Branwell had leapt into action immediately, slid the file over to him and proceeded to flick the pages.

'Branwell! What do you think you're doing? They could come back in at any moment,' she whispered urgently at him.

But he pushed her hand away from his arm and pointed at her handbag. 'For the love of God, woman, get me a piece of paper and a pen. Quickly!'

Her hands were shaking as she clumsily unclasped her bag and rummaged inside. 'Here. Hurry!' she told him, her eyes fixed on the door. 'If we get caught, I'll say it was all you.'

Branwell wrote down the contact details for Harry's son, pushed the paper and pen deep into his suit jacket, closed the file, and then placed it back in its original spot on the table.

'There. No harm done,' he said just as the door reopened and DCI Jackman and DS Hooper returned to the room.

It had been a close call – too close, and her legs had shaken with fear at the thought that somebody had been watching the camera in the interview room and had seen everything that had taken place. It wasn't until they were back in the safety of Branwell's Bentley and speeding out of the car park that she felt that she could finally breathe again.

'Well, go on then...give him a call,' instructed Branwell, but Edith shook her head at him.

'No. You do it. You sound more official than I do, and besides, you're a quick thinker. You always manage to make things sound convincing,' she replied.

He rolled his eyes back at her and pulled out his mobile phone. 'I have to say this is the most excitement I've had in years,' he said, keying in the numbers.

It started to ring out, and Branwell turned on the speakerphone and placed the mobile on the table. After only a few seconds, it was finally answered.

'Uh, hello?' a man said wearily on the other end.

'Hello. May I speak to Damien Lanscombe, please,' said Branwell in a voice even posher than his normal accent.

'Yes. Speaking,' the man they now knew to be Damien replied. 'Who is this?'

Branwell cleared his throat and leaned over the phone. 'This is Inspector Aller...that is, Alan...err...Sugar. I believe you spoke with one of my colleagues earlier?'

'Alan Sugar?' a surprised Damien said.

Edith scowled at her brother. If the best he could do was fumble his way through the conversation by offering up one of the UK's leading businessmen, they'd be rumbled in seconds.

'I know. I know,' continued Branwell. 'I get a lot of comments about the name, but I assure you I'm not the billionaire Alan Sugar. Just plain old Inspector Sugar.'

She shook her head. He was making a complete mess of this. She gave a circular motion with her hand, to hurry him along.

'Anyway. Firstly, may I offer my deepest condolences on the loss of your father,' said Branwell.

There was a pause at the end of the line. Finally, Damien responded, 'I thought your colleagues would have told you that mine and my father's relationship was fractured. I hadn't seen him in years—over twenty, at least. Condolences really aren't necessary.'

'My apologies. Force of habit,' said Branwell. 'So are you saying you never had any form of contact with your father? Not even over the telephone?'

A loud sigh travelled down the line. 'No. Again, as I explained, the last time I saw my father was just before I discovered he'd emptied my bank account and disappeared. After that, I never wanted to see him again. The man was a parasite. He used to use people all of the time, take them for what they'd had and then move on to someone else. He was like a locust.'

Edith picked up a pen, wrote on the scrap of paper, and pointed at it for Branwell to take note. He stole a quick glance and nodded back at her.

'And then, of course, there's the witness, who said that they saw you outside your father's house shortly before he was killed.'

Damien let out a loud yawn. 'And as I've told your officers, I'm not sure what drugs your witness was on because it was most definitely not me outside the door last week of wherever it was my father lived.'

'And do you have any proof of this?'

'For fuc...don't you lot liaise with each other and share information? As I told the detectives earlier, there was no way it could have been me last week because last week I was where I always am – Hong Kong, where I've lived and worked for the past three years. And no, I haven't left the country at all during this period, and yes, you're more than welcome to check my details with the immigration, or the passport office or whoever it is you need to speak to. So, if you don't mind, I'm going to hang up the phone now. It's late evening here.'

And then the line went dead.

Edith looked at her brother. 'Hong Kong? But it wasn't an international ringtone. He must be lying?'

Branwell held up his phone. 'I called him on WhatsApp.'

Edith snatched the phone from his hand, pressed on Branwell's WhatsApp profile picture and held the screen up to him. The image was of Branwell smiling broadly, his arms draped across the men standing either side of him, a bottle of beer in one hand and a rainbow feather boa dangling around his neck.

'Nothing says, Inspector, more than a pair of hotpants and feather boa,' she said sardonically.

Just then, the sound of sirens filled the air, and Edith went to the window. A convoy of police cars sped past on the road and turned at the corner.

'Come on,' she told her brother. 'We'll just have to pray that Damien doesn't say anything to anyone. Let's go and see what's going on out there. It looks serious.'

They'd followed the sounds of the sirens, taking the same turn as the police cars had done and joined the small group of villagers who were all standing in a tight huddle outside Winston Mayhew's house.

'What's going on?' she asked Brian Marston, who was whispering something into his wife's ear.

Sally Marston took Edith to the side and, in a low voice, whispered. 'They're saying that Winston's dead,' she told her. 'We heard one of the Constables talking to his wife on the phone, telling her that he was going to be late back from work that evening. He's been shot, apparently, shot straight between the eyes.'

Edith's hand went to her chest. 'Winston's dead? Do they know who did it?'

But Sally shook her head. 'Not that we've heard. But it makes you wonder, doesn't it? You never know what type of people you live next to.' She cast a suspicious glance around the crowd. 'It chills you to the bone, doesn't it? Knowing there's a serial killer on the loose in our lovely little village.'

'That's another twenty grand knocked off the house prices, I tell you,' said Brian, sidling up beside them.

'Apparently, you have to kill three people in order to be called a serial killer,' said Branwell. 'So, I wouldn't worry too much.'

Edith shook her head. Time and place, Branwell!

At that moment, a terrified Dickens was led out of the house by a uniformed officer and towards the open door of a police van.

'Excuse me?' shouted Edith. 'Where are you taking him?'

'The kennels. Where all the strays go,' the officer replied bluntly.

Edith stepped forward and snatched the lead from his hand. 'But he isn't a stray. You can't take him there, he's scared witless, the poor thing. You can't shove him in a kennel and leave him to rot.'

The officer reached out for the lead, but Edith moved her hand behind her back. 'I'll take him,' she told him. 'There's no need to take him anywhere. He can stay with me.'

The officer stepped forward towards her but was blocked by Branwell and Brian.

'We look after our own, and he,' said Brian, pointing down at the dog, 'is one of ours.'

Dickens, as if knowing he was being fought over, hunched down at Edith's feet and let out a series of small whimpers, resulting in a round of sympathetic groans from the villagers.

'See. Like I said – he's one of ours.' repeated Brian.

'Let her keep him,' Simon's voice called out.

Edith looked up and saw him and DS Hooper exiting Winston's house in full forensic gear.

'If Mrs Elliott wants to keep the dog, then so be it,' Simon continued as he removed his blue disposable gloves and dropped them in the waiting evidence bag held by one of the uniformed officers stationed in the front garden. 'Mrs Elliott always seems to know what's best.' He cut her a serious look and Edith looked away, unable to meet his eyes.

'Can you tell us what's going on?' said Branwell. 'Is Winston dead?'

Simon gave a sorry shake of his head. 'I'm afraid he is, yes,' he said and gasps of horror trickled amongst them. 'Now, if any of you have any information which you feel is useful to the investigation, can I ask you to go over to that officer over there,' he pointed behind them, and they turned to see a uniformed officer standing next to a patrol car, waving a clipboard at them.

A few people broke away from the group and headed towards the officer. Not that they had pertinent information, assumed Edith. They'd probably waste the poor man's time with nonsense, gossip and idle tittle-tattle all so they could say to the family and friends that something exciting had happened to them that day.

Simon fixed Edith, Branwell, and the Marstons with a steely glare. 'You four. Come with me,' he said sternly.

Chapter Twenty One

E mma loved working for the police – she especially loved being a detective. Nothing thrilled her more than waking up in the morning, and after a vigorous workout at the gym, jumping in the shower, getting dressed, and readying herself for what she believed would be another day fighting crime: putting bad guys behind bars and keeping the streets clean and safe for another day. But what she didn't like was waking up and going through that whole ritual only to find that her days were filled with having to deal with this type of rubbish.

Simon had just brought Edith, Branwell, Brian and Sally Marston round the side of Winston Mayhew's house through the back gate, and now they were all currently standing in the back garden looking sheepishly at one another as Simon and Emma glared back.

This was the problem when it came to solving village crime as opposed to crimes in bigger cities. As a general rule, a traditional village barely had any villainy whatsoever, save for the occasional scuffle at the pub or the odd packet of biscuits or two being spirited away from the shelves in the local supermarket.

But English villages were no longer isolated little pockets of houses hidden in the middle of the countryside. They were slowly being surrounded, encompassed and swallowed up by new, flashier housing developments, and as greedy developers snapped up every available piece of land, the once-picturesque homes were finding themselves forming part of larger estates; They were the eye in the storm of new bricks, cladding and newcomers and their once-safe little hidey-hole was now visible to every Tom, Dick and Harry. But with larger estates came increased crime, and unfortunately, the native villagers were still locked in a mindset of days which had long since vanished, where doors remained unlocked all night and where keys were indiscreetly placed under the mat on the front step.

They struggled to believe that something so heinous could happen in their community without them knowing all about it. The offender, in their opinion, had to be known to them because they, again, in their opinion, spotted everything, knew everybody, and there wasn't a single event, interaction or transaction that occurred without them noticing. They were overly keen to help, offering up theory after theory, which was tantamount to nothing more than gossip and, at times, downright slander.

During this investigation alone, the station had been inundated with villager after villager, all keen to offer up their two pennies on who they thought had killed Harry Lanscombe. One woman had even trekked the five miles to the station with her Zimmer frame to tell her that a woman called Lorraine, who worked at the Shop & Save, was definitely involved and not to be trusted as she'd once overcharged her thirty pence when she'd gone in to buy a loaf of bread and a tin of baked beans. The calibre of information wasn't just disappointing; it was a bloody hindrance.

Emma suddenly wished that she'd applied for that job at counter-terrorism now.

'Now,' said Simon sternly, 'I noticed that none of you went over to the officer to report your vital information.' He fixed each of them with a steely glare. 'Which I must say surprised me, considering I know that each of you has something that you're holding back from the police.

So, I'm going to give you one last opportunity to come clean. Otherwise, DS Hooper and I may have to look at instigating criminal charges against you all.'

Emma was impressed. Simon had done a good job reprimanding them. Brian and his wife, Sally, cast nervous glances at each other. Edith had stared back sweetly, one hand clasping the strap of her shoulder bag, the other holding Dickens's lead. She was a shrewd one, thought Emma. She gave absolutely nothing away, and you could never tell what she was thinking. Branwell, on the other hand, was an open book. His face told anybody looking all they needed to know, and at that precise second, Branwell was frankly taking the piss out of them.

'Why on earth would you think we'd know anything about anything?' he said with a chortle. He reached into his pocket, pulled out a packet of Munchies, and popped one in his mouth.

'We know that you looked at the file I left on the desk in the interview room,' said Emma. 'We had a call from Harry Lanscombe's son complaining that we were incompetent fools who needed to get their act together. After a bit of digging, we discovered what the hell he was on about. What do you have to say about that, Inspector Alan Sugar?'

Edith blanched, and not that Emma liked threatening pensioners but it was nice to see that she wasn't always able to maintain that stoic poker face of hers. She opened her mouth to say something, but Branwell nudged her in the side.

'Don't say anything, woman,' he told her. 'Here, stick a Munchie in your mouth.'

He pushed one of the chocolatey sweets into Edith's hands, which she immediately dropped on the grass. Dickens, not one to miss an opportunity, leapt to his feet and lapped it up with his tongue.

'So, if we were to check your phone right now, there wouldn't be a call to Damien Lanscombe?' continued Simon.

Branwell gave an unconcerned shrug, popped another sweet into his mouth and shook his head. 'I don't have a phone, detectives.'

At that second, the sound of Joe Cocker's, *You Can Leave Your Hat On*, blasted out from Branwell's phone that was secreted in his pocket. He retrieved it quickly, turned his back to them and answered the call.

'Now is not a good time, Geoffrey. Yes...okay. Boob tube? No, I didn't borrow it. Absolutely certain. Purple is not my colour at all. You saucy little minx,' he laughed down the phone. 'Listen. I really have to go, Geoffrey. Yep.

Talk later.' He hung up the call and turned back to them. 'Apologies. It was my accountant.'

Emma found a smile creep along her lips, and she whisked it away again. Why did Branwell have to be so annoyingly funny? In another life, outside of this village, and away from lies and the murder, she was pretty certain that she could have been friends with him.

'And you,' continued Simon, turning to the Marston's. 'We know for a fact that both of you have had more dealings with Winston Mayhew than you're letting on.'

One of Sally's hands flew to her chest; the other gripped her husband's hand. 'What on earth do you mean?'

'We've only carried out a preliminary search of Mr Mayhew's property, but I can tell you that we've found some very interesting photographs inside,' said Simon.

He was eyeballing them hard, waiting to see their reaction. Emma, on the other hand, glanced straight at Edith and Branwell to check theirs. Yep! There it was. A furtive but confused look was exchanged between them. They were probably miffed that they hadn't found the photographs themselves.

'Can we ask what the photographs pertained to?' asked Edith, to which Brian span around to face her.

'No, you bloody well can't,' he bellowed at her.

'DS Hooper,' Simon said to Emma. 'Would you mind taking Mrs Elliott and Mr Allerton back down to the station for yet another statement, which they will no doubt lie about again. I'll take Mr and Mrs Marston and take theirs.'

Emma grabbed Branwell by the arm and tugged it gently. 'Come with me please, Sir,' she told him.

He slipped another Munchie in his mouth and winked at her. 'I do love it when I'm manhandled. It's such a shame you're in plain clothes and not in uniform.'

'Or a man,' Emma replied sardonically.

'Well, yes. That too,' he replied, smiling.

Chapter Twenty Two

Edith had never even stepped foot in a police station before that day, and here she was back in the same interview room that she'd only stepped foot out of earlier that morning. If she weren't careful, she'd get a reputation for herself.

Branwell was sitting casually in the chair beside her. It astounded her how little her brother was affected by anything.

When she was first ushered to the police car, she'd lowered her head in shame as the villagers who were lingering outside Winston Mayhew's house started to mutter to each other in hushed tones, as Emma, keen to fuel the gossip, it seemed, placed a firm palm on top of Edith's head as she got into the back of the car.

Branwell, on the other hand, had completely played up to the hype and, as he was escorted into the back of the car, had shouted at the top of his voice to them all;

'I'm innocent, I tell you. Innocent!' This caused a further flurry of excitement among the onlookers.

As they sped away toward the police station, he offered the driver one of his Munchies, assuring the young PC that it was not a euphemism, nor was his offer of the chocolatey treat to be taken as a bribe.

'I know what you lot are like,' Branwell had teased. 'I've watched *Line of Duty*.'

Dickens, Edith's new ward, had taken less interest in the whole escapade and had lay down quietly in the centre seat, with his head resting on Edith's lap.

She'd always wanted a dog, she'd thought to herself, as she'd gently stroked Dickens's sleeping head. Ronnie had never let her have one. No! That was a fib, she corrected herself, remembering the time that he'd drunkenly fallen through the door with a mongrel puppy tucked under his arm, which he'd won in a bet.

She'd scooped up the frightened little animal and carried him away from Ronnie before he had the chance to stand up, fall over again and crush the thing completely. He was such a beautiful creature with his tan fur and deep conker brown eyes. With the children at school and

Ronnie safely tucked away in the corner of one of the local pubs, she'd found herself lonely as she pottered around the house, doing the same thing day in and day out. But with the dog, whom she not so imaginatively called Sandy, she felt that she had a little furry ally in the house with her to keep her sane.

Sandy kept her company in the draughty, old house and also provided her with the perfect excuse to get out of there when they all came bounding through the door in the late afternoon. She'd walk him for hours, sucking in the fresh air and daydreaming about living any other life than the one she currently had.

But Ronnie took offence to the amount of time that she was spending away from the house and out of his sight. One day, a few weeks after he'd first arrived, she came back from the shops to find that Sandy was gone.

'I left the front door open, and he bolted out the little bugger,' Ronnie had told her.

But Edith knew when he was lying; he had a habit of looking around at the ground when he spoke, and the second she saw him look to his feet, she knew that her husband had got rid of her only friend for no other reason than jealousy. She'd taken him at his word; to argue was not only pointless but downright dangerous where he was concerned, and hurried out onto the streets on the pretence of looking for Sandy. She'd gone to all of Ronnie's regular haunts: The Barrow and Boy, The Gospel Oak, The Rising Sun, and interrogated his drinking pals to see if they knew anything about the dog, but had discovered nothing and had trudged the short distance back to the house feeling utterly empty inside.

She never did find out what Ronnie had done to Sandy. She hoped he'd given him away and not hurt him—that's all Edith cared about. It had happened thirty years ago, but every so often, her little boy would appear in her mind.

Now, she had Dickens. Whether she got to keep him was another story, but try as she might, Edith just couldn't see the police issuing her with a warrant to remove him from her custody. Or could she? She and Branwell had tested DCI Jackman and DS Hooper's patience in recent days. Would they do something so petty and insist that she hand the dog over to them in accordance with whatever law they deemed fit? Maybe they should tone down their own private investigation just in case. It wasn't worth the risk, in her opinion.

'So, let me get straight to the point,' said DS Hooper. 'We've received information which states that Mr Mayhew was seen standing outside the door to your flat yesterday evening. Do you have anything to say about that?'

She looked between Edith and Branwell, fixing them with her steely green eyes.

Edith's brows crumpled with confusion as she looked over at Branwell.

'That may be the case,' said Edith. 'But he certainly never pressed the buzzer to come in.'

'Did you see him, though?' continued Emma.

Edith shook her head. 'No. Not at all,' she said diplomatically.

'Whoever told you that is lying. I suggest you go back and check your source,' said Branwell, not so diplomatically.

Edith's grip tightened on the dog lead. She wished she had one for Branwell...and a muzzle.

Sarah sighed and leaned back in the chair. 'That's the thing,' she said told them. 'It's not just one source. We've had the same account from three different witnesses. So, I'll ask you again. Did Winston Mayhew come to see you yesterday?'

'Mr Mayhew may have come to the flats, but he certainly didn't come to see us if that's the case,' said Edith. 'Isn't it possible that he went to see one of the other residents?'

But Sarah shook her head. 'Unlikely. We've checked with the tenants. One of the flats is empty, as you know. One of the tenants, Mrs Skillet, is away visiting her son in

York. And Mr Ramsey is ninety-five years old, bed-bound, and has round-the-clock care. The carers on duty that day told us that nobody visited him at all, which, by process of elimination, leaves...'

'You with a bit of problem,' finished Branwell. 'I assure you that Mr Mayhew did not press the buzzer on the security door to my sister's flat. Nor did he gain entrance by some other means and knock on her front door. We didn't see Mr Mayhew, and we didn't hear from him at all that day. As God is my witness. We're law-abiding citizens, for goodness' sake.'

Emma shot him a wry look.

'Well, we're citizens at least,' corrected Branwell.

'Exactly. You can see why DCI Jackman and myself aren't inclined to take everything you say at face value,' she told them. She gripped the pen in between her thumb and forefinger and turned it back and forth slowly as she eyed them. 'So, why should we believe you this time?'

'Because we're telling you the truth,' said Edith.

'This time,' added Branwell.

'As opposed to...' asked Emma.

'The other times when we didn t tell the truth,' he replied.

Emma stared hard at them, then jotted something down in her notebook, quite unnecessarily, in Edith's opinion.

She tilted her head to see what the sergeant had written, but Emma, spotting her looking, quickly flicked the pad closed again.

'So what happens now?' asked Edith.

'Now. You leave here. You go back home, and you stop with this silly notion of trying to solve this crime yourself. I repeat – you stop!' said Emma. 'Because if you don't, then the next time you find yourselves being brought into the station, you won't be coming in as witnesses. Do you understand what I'm telling you?'

'Absolutely. Message received loud and clear, Sergeant,' said Branwell.

Emma looked at Edith.

'We understand,' she said meekly.

Emma rose to her feet and opened the door. 'Good. Then you're free to leave,' she told them.

They stood up, but Dickens remained rooted to the spot. After a few tugs on the lead, he reluctantly stood and followed them as they walked along the corridor, through a set of security doors, and back outside to the front of the station.

'If we need anything further from you, we'll be in touch,' said Emma. 'I'd love to say that it's been a pleasure.'

'Then say it,' said Branwell. 'We're all friends here.'

But Emma shook her head with exasperation and simply closed the door in their faces. Branwell straightened his back and shrugged his shoulders.

'I think that went well,' he said, glancing down at Edith.

She sighed back at him. 'I'm glad you do,' she said as she walked down the stairs and towards the direction of the car park. 'Didn't you hear what she said? She knows that we're carrying out our own investigation. If we get caught again, we'll end up getting arrested.'

'Thrilling, isn't it?' said Branwell.

'Thrilling? All of these years that I haven't seen you, and I've not been arrested once. You've been back in my life for a couple of weeks, and I've practically got my own interview room.'

He went over to his Bentley, held the handle, and it clunked as it unlocked. Cars were so clever nowadays, marvelled Edith.

'Would you have it any other way, sister dearest?'

'Actually. Yes. I would. I'd have it that I lived in a world where we weren't threatened with receiving a prison term,' she opened the back door for Dickens, and he jumped onto the backseat and assumed his sleeping position immediately.

'Please don't tell me that you're having second thoughts?' panicked Branwell as he got into the car. 'We're getting close. I can feel it.'

Edith slid into the passenger seat beside him. 'Second thoughts? Are you crazy? Not on your nelly. I know that we've already seen the answer to all of this wickedness. It's there somewhere, in the depths of our brains. We just don't know that we've seen it yet.'

'Good girl,' he said, patting her leg. 'You had me worried then. Where to now?'

He started the car, and the engine rumbled softly. 'Do you know, after all that unpleasantness, I'm feeling like I could do with a nice cold drink.' She turned to him and smiled.

'Pub?' he suggested.

'Pub,' she replied bluntly.

Chapter Twenty Three

Simon silently flicked through the photographs in the interview room, strategically looking up every so often at Brian and Sally Marston before shaking his head and focusing his attention back on the photos. When he was suitably satisfied that he'd tortured them enough, he lowered each photo on the desk, laying them out in a neat line for them to see. Brian and Sally leaned in to take a closer look. Brian's face contorted with rage as he viewed them, and Sally promptly burst into tears.

'Oh, God. No,' she blubbed as her eyes settled on them.

There, in all their glory, were images of the loving couple dressed head to toe in tight, unforgiving PVC outfits. In Sally's hand, she clasped a whip as Brian bent over on the bed, eagerly awaiting the punishment that his wife was about to deliver. The photo, owing to the fact that it had secretly been taken without their knowledge through their bedroom window, was a little blurry, but their images and the content were unmistakable. Why didn't people close their curtains anymore? Simon thought to himself with dismay. They'd save themselves a whole heap of trouble if they just took the few seconds it needed to protect themselves from such ridicule. But as he thought this, he gave himself a mental slap around the head. He'd already gone to the pub to check out the viewing position. Winston must have had to have climbed over the back fence and into the pub's beer garden, scaled the brick wall that lined the border, and then clambered up the branches of the old Oak tree in order to find the right position to take the photos. Mr Mayhew, God rest his soul, had had more stamina than Simon did – he pulled a muscle in his groin doing a simple drunken cartwheel in his brother's garden at last summer's barbeque.

'What can you tell me about these?' he asked the pair.

'What do you want me to tell you about them? It's quite clear what's happening, or do you coppers lead sheltered lives nowadays?' Brian snapped back.

'Did you know that Mr Mayhew had taken them?'

Brian glared at Simon as though he'd just asked him to eat a newborn baby. 'Are you insane? Do you think I'd let that old perv's eyeballs anywhere near my Sally?'

'Did he tell you that he had them?' continued Simon.

'Of course he didn't,' sniffed Sally as she dabbed her eyes with a tissue.

Brian remained silent, and Simon stared at him. 'Is that correct, Mr Marston? You weren't aware that Mr Mayhew had compromising pictures of you and your wife together?'

Brian looked down at his hands and clasped his hands together. 'Listen. He may have said ..implied something the other day in the beer garden.'

'What?' said Sally, as her hand flew to cover her mouth.

'And what exactly did he imply?' pressed Simon.

Brian fumbled with his fingers, unable to lift his head to meet the gazes of Simon and Sally.

'I was moaning about the motorcycles that speed through the village to everybody at the bar the other day, and he said...he said that he was surprised I had such an issue with it considering how much I liked to wear leather. And then he sort of winked and smiled...you know? Like he was enjoying himself,' said Brian.

This was more like it, thought Simon. Finally, it felt as though he was getting somewhere.

'And what did you do?' he asked Brian.

Brian covered his face with his hands and began to weep.

This is it! He's on the verge of crumbling, Simon silently thought. Any second now, he'll confess, and that's it – case closed. However, he could hardly blame Brian for losing his temper and popping off Winston, given the explosive information he had on them. Something like that would destroy a reputation completely in a backward village such as theirs, and if it had all come out, then they would have had to leave the pub, their home, and their friends, and all because one old man couldn't keep his camera in his pocket, so to speak.

'Mr Marston?' he asked again. 'What did you do?'

Brian turned to his wife and pulled her into a tight hug. 'Nothing. I did nothing! I was too stunned...too scared to say anything. I just wandered away from the bar, feeling as though my heart was about to leap out of my chest.'

'So just to confirm,' said Simon. 'You didn't do anything?'

'Well, not exactly. I didn't charge him for his steak and kidney pie and chips,' replied Brian.

Simon sighed and ran a hand through his hair in exasperation. 'No. I mean – you didn't threaten him? Or hurt him? Or go to his house and shoot him in the head?

That sort of thing. I'm not talking about letting him off with paying for his lunch.'

Brian looked up at Simon through teary eyes. 'Shoot him? What do you think this place is? The O.K. Corral?'

'Tell me you didn't, Brian,' implored Sally. 'Tell me you didn't kill him?' She clung to his t-shirt and pushed her head into his chest.

'Kill him? You daft mare!' said Brian, pushing her away from him and staring into her eyes. 'You think I'd risk everything we have for some old deviant who gets his kicks spying on people? No. Of course I didn't kill him. But...'

Simon moved in closer. 'But?'

'But I did try to break into his house last night. I was going to sneak in and take the pictures...and that wretched camera of his. But when I went round to the back of the house and peered in through the living room curtains, I saw him – sitting there.' Brian burst into a fresh wave of tears. 'But he was already dead. So I got out of there as fast as I could.'

As Brian and Sally consoled each other, Simon leaned back and observed them. His mind raced with a thousand theories. Brian could be lying. It's quite possible that he did go to Winston Mayhew's house, found his gun, and shot him with it. Equally, it was possible for Brian to have killed Harry Lanscombe too. He certainly had beef with the man, and let's not forget that he only had to slip behind the marquee panel behind the bar for a second or two to carry out the deed. Yes, there were plenty of people in there who swore that Brian had been present in the tent for the entire time, but could they really be certain? It would only have taken him a second or two to slip out unnoticed when everyone's backs were turned, pummel Harry in the head and slip back in again.

But the more Simon looked at Brian Marston, the less comfortable he felt about the whole thing. Something just didn't seem right. Brian may have been a big lump of a man, but the photos seemed to prove the opposite. He was submissive and under his wife's control—at least, he was in the bedroom. No. Brian Marston, nor his wife, Sally, fit in this whole sorry debacle.

'Interview terminated at three-fifteen p.m.' He stood sharply. 'I'll send PC Harris in to get your statements. You're free to go...for now,' he added, feeling that he ought to remind them that they weren't completely off the hook just yet.

He started to collect the photographs, shuffling them into one pile.

'Do you have to keep those?' asked Sally, pointing down at the photos.

Simon picked them up and slid them into the file in his hand. 'Yes. I'm afraid we do.'

'Shame,' she said, looking thoughtful. 'There's a couple of decent shots of me in there.'

Chapter Twenty Four

Edith and Branwell had been sitting in the far corner of the bar of the Ewe and Lamb for almost three hours, next to the roaring log fire, which had bizarrely been lit even though it was a sweltering twenty-three degrees outside. Not bad for England, thought Edith. It must have something to do with that climate crisis that they keep harping on about on the news.

Branwell wasn't faring too well in the heat. Beads of sweat ran down his face, dripping off his chin and plopped down into his glass of wine. He'd managed to last almost an hour, sitting in his suit and suffering in sweaty silence, until he'd finally admitted defeat and removed his suit jacket, draping it over the back of the chair. Twenty minutes later, he'd removed his waistcoat, and Edith had only stepped in when she caught him unbuttoning his shirt.

'I don't think so, Branwell,' she told him sternly.

'What's the problem? I'm wearing a vest. It's not like the patrons will be subjected to the sight of my nipples.'

Unfortunately for them, word of Brian and Sally's visit to the station had whizzed through the village like a whirlwind, and the entire pub was packed to the rafters, all keen to hear the gossip from them when they returned. There wasn't a seat spare in the entire place, and Edith and Branwell had thought themselves lucky when they'd spotted the free small round table tucked away in the far corner of the bar, next to the inglenook fireplace. After five minutes of sitting there, they realised why everybody had veered clear of sitting there.

After an hour and a half, Branwell rose from his seat, reached over to the wood burner and closed the vents. The fire dimmed until, eventually, and much to their relief, it extinguished completely.

'Good grief, they are a backwards lot here, aren't they?' he said as he dabbed his forehead with a handkerchief. 'I don't know how much longer I can sit here, Edith. I truly don't.'

Edith reached over and patted his hand. 'I'll get you another drink,' she told him.

She went to the bar, returning a few minutes later with a pint of ice-cold beer. Branwell wrinkled his nose at the sight of the amber liquid but took the glass from her hands anyway and, upon feeling the coldness of the drink against his fingers, gulped half of the pint down within seconds.

'Oh my,' he said, wiping his lips with the back of his hand. 'Keep those coming.'

Finally, Brian and Sally Marston walked back into the pub to raucous applause from the villagers. Brian gave a broad smile, holding his hands in the air as though he'd just been released from a twenty-year prison sentence following a miscarriage of justice.

Sally, on the other hand, sheepishly looked down at her feet, scuttled behind the bar and poured herself a liberal measure of neat vodka from the optics.

Brian thumbed Barry Gosling from his chair and clambered up. 'And to celebrate, the drinks are on us!' he announced at the top of his voice, resulting in a fresh round of cheers.

'Only one,' added Sally, 'and single measures only if you're having shorts.' But her words were lost amongst the racket.

Branwell immediately stood up, polished off the remaining contents of his now third pint of beer, and pushed his way through the crowd and to the front of the bar. Edith rolled her eyes; he never was one to turn down a free drink.

They remained at the pub for a further three hours. Edith yawned loudly, twisting her empty glass around on the table. So far, she'd had two glasses of wine and three port and lemons – much more than she was used to drinking, and she could feel a gentle fuzziness spreading across her body as the alcohol took its effect.

Branwell, despite having had seven pints in total, was far more coherent than she expected him to be. Edith had already dipped her hand into his suit jacket and removed his car keys, just in case he got some silly notion to drive himself home. However, she was slightly perturbed at the thought of him stopping over at her flat for the night. There was no way he'd be able to squeeze himself onto her tiny two-seater without dislocating a couple of joints, and seeing as there was only one bedroom, it meant that she and Branwell would have to share a bed.

The only person Edith had ever shared a bed with had been Ronnie, and he'd been dead for years. She'd grown quite used to sleeping starfish on her back, not caring if she was snoring loudly now that there was nobody else for her to worry about waking. Oh lord, what if Branwell snored like a pig snuffling for truffles? She wouldn't get a wink of sleep all night, she thought selfishly. In saying that, she reasoned, they'd both drank back quite a lot of booze, so with any luck, they'd both fall into a drunken coma and sleep soundly.

If they didn't get to speak to Brian and Sally alone soon, Edith doubted that they'd even make it back to the flat that night. There were only a few stragglers left now, the others having left seemingly satisfied after the free drink and a snippet of tittle-tattle from the hosts.

Sally was busy collecting the empty glasses from the tables as Brian disappeared down into the cellar to replace the now empty barrel of bitter thanks to his earlier generosity.

Edith nudged her brother in the ribs, and he lifted his head and narrowed his eyes somewhat unsteadily as Sally neared their table.

'It's good that the local constabulary saw sense and let you go,' he said to Sally as she reached their table.

She smiled sweetly at him and hooked her fingers into the several empty glasses littering their table. 'Yes. Well, I suppose they had nothing on us, so it's hardly surprising.'

Branwell blew out his cheeks. 'I wouldn't quite say they had nothing,' he said, giving her a cheeky wink. 'Not from what I saw anyway.'

Sally looked around cautiously. 'You saw them?' she asked with surprise.

'Just a few of them,' said Branwell. 'I came across them the other day at Winston's when the old man was alive and kicking.'

Sally pulled out a chair and sat down next to them. 'He was a disgraceful person if you ask me,' she whispered to them both as she leaned across the table. 'What two consenting adults get up to in their bedroom is nobody's business except theirs. Although, there is something quite...' she paused, trying to formulate the right word, 'alluring, about being watched.'

Edith pulled back her lips in disgust. Not that she was ever one to judge another person, but there were certain things that she would just never understand, and voyeurism was right up there at the top of her very extensive list.

'And Winston never said anything to you about it all?' she asked Sally.

Sally shook her head. 'Not once. We didn't have a clue. Although, Brian admitted at the station that Winston had hinted something to him about knowing.'

'Whether you did or didn't know is irrelevant, I suppose,' added Branwell. 'After all, you both had watertight alibis for the night of Winston's murder, I assume?'

Sally retreated back in her seat, and focused her attention on the glasses. 'Yes, of course. We were at home all night.'

'And neither of you left at any point during the evening?' asked Edith.

'No. Not at all,' replied Sally. 'Brian ran me a lovely warm bubble bath – he put rose petals in it and everything. And while I chilled in there for an hour or so, he cooked us a lovely beef bourguignon from scratch, too! He really treated me that evening. And then after that, we had...fun...together.'

Edith downed the last of her port and lemon and handed the empty glass over to Sally, keen not to encourage Sally to start divulging yet more of her and her husband's sexscapades.

'Well, all's well that ends well,' she said to Sally, and then turning to Branwell she motioned with her head for them to leave.

Once outside, Branwell slid his arms into his shirt and began to button it up. 'Why the rush?' he asked Edith. 'She was starting to open up then.'

'No. She told us everything we needed to know and was about to start telling us about a whole lot of stuff that we most definitely *didn't* need to know. Anyway, I want to check something out. Come with me.'

Edith went around the side of the building, across the car park and nudged open the fenced enclosure which hid the pub's trash bins.

'You start looking through that one,' she told Branwell as she lifted the lid on one of the bins.

Branwell gagged as the pungent scent of rotten food, fermented by the warm weather, attacked his nostrils.

'You're on your own with this one, you mad cow,' he told her. 'What are you looking for anyway?' he added as he pinched his nostrils closed with his thumb and forefinger.

Edith held her breath as she tore open one of the black bags and riffled through the contents. It was a good job that she was drunk; sober Edith wouldn't dare do something like this.

As she continued to rummage, her watery eyes widened, and she plucked out exactly what she'd been searching for.

'This,' she said, holding the offending cardboard wrapper in her hands.

'Good god, woman. Exactly how much have you had to drink?' said Branwell.

Branwell had eaten two rounds of toast, downed a glass of water and promptly flopped into Edith's bed wearing only his boxer shorts and vest. She could hear his snoring reverberating around the flat and straight into the living room, and she'd found herself turning up the television to an eardrum-piercing volume twenty. She'd decided to sleep in the living room that night, knowing that no amount of alcohol would see her through a night of having to sleep next to that racket.

She unfurled the spare blanket and plumped up the pillow in the corner. If she scrunched up her knees to her chest, she could just about fit her body on the sofa – whether she'd be able to move the next morning without wincing in pain was another matter.

'It's been an odd sort of day, Ron,' she said to the googly-eyed urn as she shuffled her body into a more comfortable position. 'You know me, I'm not one to drink too much, but I've had one after the other today. You'd have been proud of me if you saw me. Okay, maybe not the part when I stumbled into the bushes in Mrs Patterson's garden, but the rest of it, you'd have definitely been surprised.'

She looked at the urn, allowing the non-existent conversation to take place.

'I know! That was a right turn up for the books, wasn't it?' she continued, as though 'urn' Ronnie had asked her a question. 'It was just a hunch, that was all. You know how that sort of thing used to drive you mad when you'd been here because it basically meant that you couldn't get away with anything. But I remembered a while ago when the chef, Dorcas, was off sick with a stomach bug. Sally had caught it too – I'm not one to gossip, but she and Dorcas were always pretty close, if you know what I mean. Anyway, Brian had been forced to cook in the kitchens that day, and it was chaos, absolute, utter chaos. The only thing that managed to come out of the kitchen that day had been an unfortunate dose of salmonella, which a few of the locals didn't thank him for, let me tell you. And then I remembered after the environmental health had finished their investigation, Brian mentioned that he couldn't cook to save his life – which was clearly evident. So, when Sally mentioned that he'd cooked her a beef bourguignon from scratch, I knew that he had to have been lying.'

Edith's eyes drifted to the beef bourguignon cardboard wrapper, now safely sealed in a Ziplock freezer bag normally reserved for leftover meals.

'Exactly,' she said to the silent question that urn Ron had asked her in her mind. 'Why did he lie about making it himself? That is the question! It all seems a little premeditated, don't you think? Yes, I do too. Brian got Sally out of the way by running her a romantic bath while he was allegedly cooking their dinner when, in actual fact, he'd pinged it for five minutes in the microwave, and she had no idea where he was in the flat. His alibi is worthless.'

She looked up at the urn. 'Yes, I know I'll have to let the police know, and I will, first thing in the morning when I'm less tipsy.'

She paused again.

'No, I won't forget,' she snapped.

Pause.

'Now, there's no need to say things like that, is there?'

Pause.

'I'm tired now, Ron. Night night,' she told the urn.

She'd ideally liked to have slept facing away from him. Edith had never slept facing Ronnie in all the years they had been married, but the sofa's constraints meant that she'd have to break both of her legs if she wanted to change position. Considering she was warm and snuggly underneath the blanket, she decided that this once, she'd let it slide. Within minutes, Edith was fast asleep and snoring as loudly as Branwell.

Chapter Twenty Five

Simon put the phone back in the cradle and looked at Emma, who was busy reapplying her lipstick for the umpteenth time.

'Well, that was interesting,' he said to her.

Emma smacked her lips together and double-checked the result in the mirror before dropping the mirror and the lipstick back into her handbag.

'What was it about?'

'Anonymous tip-off. Guess what about?' he said teasingly.

Emma sighed loudly. 'The King abdicated? Christ almighty. It could be about anything. Just tell me.'

'A concerned citizen has just told me that they saw a gun at Felicity Horsfall's house.'

He sat back in his chair and narrowed his eyes. Try as he might, he just couldn't imagine that woman handling a gun, let alone firing one.

'Who tipped you off?' asked Emma, whose face mirrored Simon's unconvinced expression.

He shrugged his shoulders. 'That's sort of covered with the word anonymous,' he replied flatly.

Emma picked up her stress ball, a Secret Santa present from some unimaginative soul in the station last year, and threw it at Simon.

'I know that, Smartarse. But did you recognise the voice?' she admonished.

Simon rubbed the side of his head where the ball hit him – those things were bloody heavier than they looked.

'I couldn't even tell if it was a man or a woman. They did a good job of concealing their voice, so no. I've no idea,' he said.

'Might be a hoax?' said Emma.

'Humm. Might be,' agreed Simon. He nibbled the end of his pen, his eyes fixed on nothing in particular. 'But we should still go and check it out. A lead is a lead, after all. Come on.'

He stood up and pushed his arms into his coat.

'Aren't you going to organise the armed response unit?' asked Emma, but Simon shook his head.

'Nah. It might be a hoax, like you said. But get on the phone and get me a warrant, will you? We'll give the house a good going over just in case.'

Emma nodded back at him and picked up the phone on her desk to organise the warrant.

There was something odd about all of this business that niggled away at Simon. Something which he couldn't quite put his finger on. The leads were coming in, he wouldn't quite say thick and fast, but they were coming in nonetheless. But every lead had resulted from a tip-off or a piece of gossip accidentally spilt by one of the villagers. It wasn't that he and his team hadn't found their own evidence, of course they had, but it was more that Simon felt he was slowly being pushed in a direction. It wasn't the natural flow that usually came from an investigation, where one piece of information led them to another, until eventually, they found themselves at the point of conclusion.

This sensation was completely different to that. It was as though he was being manipulated by an unseen hand. Simon could sense the outside force interweaving themself into every twist and turn. But who? Who could it be? And how could they be so devious, so unassuming, that it blinkered Simon from even realising who it was?

In all his years of policing, he'd never known anything like it. He couldn't wait for the whole thing to be over so that he could shake the draconian buildings and villagers off his clothes and hair. Maybe he'd take a break when he'd solved the case. Somewhere hot and sunny, and where the beer was cheap and the cigarettes even cheaper. Yes, a Greek island seemed to be calling to him. He loved the cuisine and the food and the whole lazy, laid-back feel that sunshine-filled holidays always gave. He'd have to check and see if any of his mates were available – he couldn't go on his own. Gosh, no. Simon wasn't one of those people who could go jet-setting alone. He just wouldn't feel comfortable with that at all! Lone travellers always looked a bit seedy, or maybe that was just his policeman's mind working overtime? Not everybody who went through the airport on their own had a kilo of heroin stashed in the lining of their suitcase.

As Emma made the arrangements on the phone, his thoughts drifted to Edith and Branwell. Was it possible that either of them had something to do with the tip-off? Actually, yes, it was highly possible. They'd ingrained themselves deep into the investigation. And thinking about it, they'd been to Winston Mayhew's house and removed evidence, which they then brought to the station on the provision that they were given something in return.

And not content with being told no and threatened with criminal proceedings, they'd peeked at a confidential file and got what they'd come for anyway. That bloody pair will be the death of him. But how involved were they exactly? Was it just a case of fancying themselves as amateur sleuths, as Emma believed? Or was it something more sinister than that? Were they actually orchestrating the whole thing?

He shook the feeling away. It wasn't helpful for him to think about those two right now. He needed to go to Felicity Horsfall's home and check things over. If he'd ignored the tip-off just because he believed it to be somebody's idea of a sick joke, and it turned out that Ms Horsfall was indeed an ageing murderess, then there'd be hell to pay, and Simon could kiss goodbye to that Greek island that he had fixed in his mind.

After he'd finished at the Horsfall woman's house, as a precaution, maybe he'd pay Edith and Branwell a visit and make sure that they were keeping in line.

Emma bounded up the path like she was about to take out a gang of football hooligans, and Simon chuckled at her overzealous enthusiasm. Didn't she realise she was about to hammer on the door of a woman who baked cakes for a living? Unless Felicity Horsfall was wielding an electric whisk in their direction when she answered the door, he doubted that there was much need for Emma's aggression.

Emma slammed her fist on the door regardless, and a somewhat bemused Ms Horsfall answered it wearing an apron, clutching a wooden spoon, and with a nose covered in what Simon hoped was flour and not a class-A drug.

'Ms Horsfall, we have a warrant to search this property,' declared Emma, flashing the warrant in her face.

She pushed a speechless Felicity to one side and barged into the house, with Simon and eight police officers following behind.

'And what exactly are you looking for?' said Felicity as one of the PCs plucked the offending spoon from her hand and placed it on the sideboard.

'We've received information that states that you have a firearm somewhere on the property,' Emma said sternly, to which Felicity laughed.

'A firearm? Sweetheart, I've never even seen a gun in my life, let alone own one, but please, feel free to take a look for yourself.'

Simon's heart sank. He had a knack for knowing when someone was telling him the truth, and Felicity, with her blasé composure, oozed honesty. Still, seeing as they'd come this far, they may as well see it through.

'If you'd like to go with one of my officers, we'll try and get this over and done with as quickly as possible,' he told her.

Felicity rolled her eyes and whipped off her apron, flinging it across the sofa.

'Knock yourself out,' she told them, walking out of the house and into the front garden and to where a small group of villagers, having seen the numerous police cars whizzing along the roads with their flashing lights, had set up camp on the pavement behind the small hedgerow.

'Right. You four upstairs. You two check out the kitchen, and you two search the back garden. DS Hooper and I will take the living room,' instructed Simon.

Heavy boots thudded up the stairs, and a series of clunks and the dragging of furniture sounded through the floorboards above their heads.

'What you feeling?' Emma asked Simon. 'Is that Mary Berry vibe she's giving out an act? Or do you think she's Calamity Jane incarnate?'

'I'm more inclined to go with the Mary Berry,' said Simon as he pulled open one of the sideboard drawers. Inside was a mass of paperwork, mainly unpaid bills. 'It looks like she was in a right mess,' he continued, holding up one of the final demands for Emma to see.

He continued rummaging as Emma knelt by the television unit and started pulling out the DVDs.

'Check this out,' she said, giving a long whistle. 'Fifty Shades of Grey, Eyes Wide Shut and Kama Sutra. Honestly, this lot are a randy bunch! Remind me to *definitely* move somewhere like this when I retire.'

Simon pulled back his lips in a grimace. 'I'd rather be celibate than live somewhere like this. Everybody seems to know everybody else's business. It'd drive me mad.'

'They don't know everything,' replied Emma. 'If they did, this investigation would have been over long ago.'

As Simon moved on to the next drawer, his stomach let out a loud growl, and his thoughts turned to that night's dinner. He was supposed to meet Andy for the darts tournament at their local pub, but a local pub meant beer and a greasy pub meal, most probably a burger, seeing as it was the only thing on the menu that didn't taste like burnt rubber. But he looked down at his bulging tummy, which now extended over his belt, and decided against it. He really needed to try and get some of this mid-life weight off his waistline. If he were going to enter the world of online dating, then he should at least try to look his best.

'Sir,' he heard Emma say, breaking his thoughts.

Simon turned to find Emma holding the handle of an upturned gun between two fingers. 'Some hoax, eh?' she said.

Chapter Twenty Six

Edith gulped down another glass of water and steadied herself against the kitchen counter. That was the reason she didn't drink a lot, she reminded herself, rubbing her temple with her finger as though it would somehow magic the hangover away.

Branwell, in contrast, breezed out of her bedroom impeccably dressed and bright-eyed.

'Oh dear, Edie,' he said, looking down at her with dismay. 'You look like shit.'

'You always know the right words to make a woman feel good about herself,' she replied, taking another sip of water.

'I'd blame the lime you add to your lager. It's the syrup—far too much sugar,' he added as he boiled the kettle.

'Of course, the syrup. Silly me. Nothing whatsoever to do with the alcohol,' she replied.

'Take it from an expert,' replied Branwell. 'Next time, leave off the stuff and see what difference it makes. Anyway, with the amount of money in your bank account, surely you could afford something with a little more class?'

He held up an empty mug and wiggled it in Edith's face. Edith nodded.

'Yes, please,' she said. There was only so much water she could tolerate.

'So, when are you going to start spending like the millionaire you are? I mean, this flat is lovely and all that, but you should definitely think about upsizing. At least think about buying somewhere with a second bedroom.'

Edith sighed and shook her aching head at him. 'I couldn't leave Hinklebury. I love it here...apart from the murders, of course.'

Branwell let out a loud scoff. 'You love the murders, admit it,' he said. 'Anyway, who said anything about leaving? I hear there's a lovely three-bedroom about to come onto the market.'

He held out the mug of steaming tea and Edith took it from his hands. 'Oh? Where?'

'Well, it's not like Winston will need it now.'

Edith tutted and tapped him on the arm. 'You vulture. The man isn't even buried yet.'

'No,' said Branwell, taking a tentative sip from his own cup. 'But he will be soon, so you should act fast.'

They went into the living room and sat down.

'Why don't you ask Ronald what he thinks?' he asked, pointing at the urn. 'I heard you talking to him last night. Do you do that a lot?'

She felt an involuntary burn in her cheeks and looked away. 'I bet you think I'm crazy, don't you?'

'For talking to your dead husband in his urn? Oh no, Edith. I thought you were crazy long before that,' replied Branwell, smiling warmly at her.

As much as it pained Edith to admit that her brother was right, she had to agree that a second bedroom would come in useful, not just for Branwell to stay in but also when Sunny came up to visit her. And now she also had Dickens to consider. A little garden would come in handy during bad weather or if she was too ill to take him for a walk one of the days. But Winston Mayhew's home? Wouldn't it be considered uncouth to buy his house, especially now that she'd taken possession of his dog? She could hear the jibes of the other villagers now, calling her Winston as a joke – minus the illicit photograph-taking and perverse voyeurism, obviously.

'Let's talk about it another time,' said Edith, keen to change the subject. 'We need to start afresh. We're missing something, Branwell, but I'm not sure what.'

Branwell set down his cup on the coffee table. 'Do you know what we haven't done?' he said to her. 'We haven't gone to the victim's homes and had a mooch around. Maybe we'll spot something the police have missed?'

Edith glanced at him unconvincedly. 'The police will scrutinise everything inside the houses. They won't miss a thing.'

But Branwell brushed her comments away with a flick of his hand. 'No. They'll be looking for blood, fingerprints, bullets, and whatnot. I'm talking about the little things; things that would make sense to you, seeing as you knew both men far better than they did. And besides, you see things most normal humans miss completely.'

Edith smiled. 'And how do you suggest we gain access? Just walk up to the door and ask for them to let us inside?'

He rubbed his hands together and smiled deviously. 'Not quite, sister mine. Not quite.'

'This is completely illegal, Branwell. DCI Jackman was

quite clear about what would happen to us if he caught us again,' whispered Edith.

She knelt beside him at the keyhole of Harry Lanscombe's front door. The police had long since finished their forensic investigation there, the only tell-tale sign of their presence being the police tape, which criss-crossed the front door.

'What on earth have you got there?' she asked, staring at the minuscule tools in his hands.

'It's my professional safe-breaking kit,' he whispered back to her. 'Now, shush. You're putting me off.'

'Why would you have a professional safe-breaking kit?'

He lowered his hands and looked at Edith. 'It's a funny story, actually,' he said, his eyes glistening at the memory. 'I was once caught in a rather compromising situation with a member of the aristocracy...and when I say aristocracy, I mean royalty,' he winked at her. 'Anyway, the pictures that were taken for our pleasure had somehow found their way into the hands of a hideous and devious spiff on the prowl for a payout; the cheeky bugger. Anyway, long story short...'

'Enough,' said Edith, holding up the palm of her hand in his face. 'Just get on with it.'

The sound of *This Morning* from Elsie's television in the neighbouring flat echoed around the empty corridor.

'Almost there,' said Branwell. 'And if I just – '

The door lock clicked open. Branwell, still on his knees, pushed the door open wide and held out his hand for Edith to pass.

'Ladies first,' he said smugly.

Her knee crunched disconcertedly as she rose to her feet, and she scurried inside, pushing the door closed after Branwell entered.

The air in the flat was freezing, and the smell of dampness lingered all around them.

'It's so chilly in here,' said Branwell. 'Old Harry mustn't have used the heating for months.'

Edith slowly nodded her head in silent agreement. 'That's no surprise given what we know about him.'

They went into the bedroom and peeked inside the wardrobe and drawers of the sideboard: nothing. Nor was anything underneath the bed save for a dusty old suitcase filled with black-and-white photographs, which, judging from the clothes, dated back as far as the Victorian era.

The kitchen was spotlessly clean except for the black smudges of carbon on surfaces and doorframes, which the forensics team had left. Inside the cupboards, they found neat rows of tinned food, each in its own category: carrots, peas, soup, and far too many tins of potatoes than was necessary.

'It has a *Sleeping with the Enemy* vibe, don't you think?' said Branwell as he viewed the tinned food with disdain. 'How anybody could eat that stuff is beyond me.'

'I'm not sure the State Retirement Pension stretches to Foie Gras,' said Edith sarcastically.

Branwell rolled his eyes, entered the living room, and opened the cupboard of a ridiculously large unit that swamped the small room. Edith glanced around at the few photographs he had displayed. One of Harry as a much younger man, dating back to the sixties judging from the clothes he was wearing, and another one taken years later, but still taken many years ago, where Harry, two stone lighter and with far less wrinkles, had his arms draped across the shoulder of an imposing man with a purple punk rocker mohawk.

'This must be Damien,' she said quietly, staring at the smiling images of Harry and his son.

'Hello. What do we have here?' he said, pulling out a plastic folder. 'It seems that Harry boy had more than his state pension being deposited into his account.'

Edith replaced the photograph and shuffled up beside him. Her eyes widened at the balance. 'Why was he so tight with his money when he had all of that?'

'Edie, he had all of that *because* he was so tight,' Branwell replied flatly.

He sat down on the armchair and continued leafing through the file. 'Do you know anybody who works at the bank?' he asked her.

'There's Maureen; she's worked there for years,' she replied.

'Do you think she'll tell us anything if we went in and asked her a couple of questions?'

Maureen was as discreet as a foghorn, as Edith thought back to the time Maureen had caught the old bank manager, Edward Mattison, depositing more than just cheques in the safe when it came to one of the younger clerks a couple of years ago. Maureen had backed out of the safe unseen, mumbled something about a family emergency to a colleague, and proceeded straight to the Ewe and Lamb, where she told everybody in there exactly what she had seen.

The news reached Edward Mattison's wife before Maureen had even left the pub, and before you could say 'account closed,' she'd left her cheating husband, taking the brand new Mercedes, their pet Labradoodle, and several of Edward's credit cards with her.

'I'd be surprised if she hasn't already blabbed anyway,' said Edith. 'Come on. We really should get out of here. It feels wrong to rifle through a dead man's belongings.'

Branwell stood up and brushed away a deluge of crumbs from his trousers. 'Yes. You've still got another one to go, so don't relax just yet,' he told her.

Accessing Winston Mayhew's house had been far easier than it had to get into Harry's. Although the police had finished searching the house, a lowly constable stood on patrol outside the front door. It was the same PC who Edith had snatched Dickens's lead from after Winston had first been murdered.

When his eyes first settled on Edith and Branwell as they approached the door, Edith copped his eyebrows, crumpling with dismay. Their last interaction had been somewhat fraught, but she decided that the nicely-nicely approach would be in order this time.

'I'm sorry to bother you when you're so busy,' she told the constable. 'But apparently, Dickens here is supposed to have daily medication for his arthritis.'

She looked down at the dog, who, in response, wagged his tail and jumped up her side excitedly; she'd have to have strong words with him later for letting her down.

The PC looked down at the dog and then back up at Edith. 'He seems okay to me,' he said flatly.

'But that's because his pills are still in his system,' interrupted Branwell. 'Give it another day, and the poor thing won't be able to cock his leg, and then where will we be?'

'In a bit of a mess, I'd say,' said the PC without a hint of concern.

'Come on, old chap. Show a bit of compassion,' added Branwell. 'If we could just have his meds, we'll get out of your way. I mean, it's not the dog's fault now, is it?'

The constable let out a heavy sigh. 'I'm not supposed to leave the front door. I'm afraid I can't help you.'

Edith stepped forward. 'Of course, and we wouldn't want you to get in any trouble. If we could go in, we can whizz around and be out again before you know it.'

Edith could see he was wavering, so she took another step closer. 'There's nobody around to see—honestly, in and out. Nobody will ever know that we've been inside,' she said, lowering her voice.

The constable looked around at the deserted street and huffed. 'Fine. But be quick,' he said, stepping aside. 'Two minutes, and then I'm coming to get you.'

Edith bristled and hurried through the front door, practically dragged forward by an enthused Dickens who was happy to be back in familiar surroundings.

Much like Harry Lanscombe's, everything in the house was neat, tidy, and ordered. There was no clutter to speak of and no obvious clue to anybody other than Winston having been there.

'Single men are much more fastidious than I expected them to be,' she said to her brother, who chuckled in response.

'Not me, Edie. If it weren't for the cleaners at Althorp Hall, it'd look like an episode of *Hoarders*, I assure you,' he replied.

In the living room, where Winston had been shot, the armchair had been removed, presumably by the police for a more thorough forensic examination, but the tell-tale signs of it having been there remained with the square of pristine, untrodden carpet, which it had once covered.

'What's this?' said Branwell.

He crouched by the armchair's original resting place and plucked small grains from the carpet.

'Sand? he said, crumbling it between his fingers and letting it drop back to the floor. 'Why would there be sand inside the house?' Had he been away anywhere?'

Edith shook her head. 'Not that I'm aware of,' she told him as she scanned the mantlepiece. 'I remember him telling everybody at one of the pub quizzes that he'd travelled enough while in the army.'

'Is there anywhere in the village that has sand? A sand pit for children, perhaps?' asked Branwell. 'Or maybe it came from the murderer's shoes? Ingrained in the tread. They could be having garden work done or something.'

'Perhaps,' said Edith, absentmindedly as she picked up a photograph of Winston and his wife, Mabel, on their wedding day. Their two smiling faces beamed back at her, and she smiled down at them. How strange to think how quickly a person's life could change and be obliterated from society as though they never really mattered. Eventually, there'd be nobody left on the planet to remember them, and it'd be as though they never really existed in the first place; life could be cruel like that.

'We should go,' said Edith, replacing the photograph on the shelf. 'We've been longer than two minutes. We don't want the constable to come and find us mooching around.'

Edith took one final glance around the room, thinking about how her possessions would look in the room, and she whipped the imaginary décor away again. Too soon, Edith, too soon.

'Did you find them?' asked the constable as they stepped back outside.

'Unfortunately, not,' she replied. 'We didn't find a thing.'

And they scuttled back up the garden path and made their way to the bank.

Chapter Twenty Seven

Emma had pulled up outside Edith's flat with the sole intention of what exactly? She had absolutely no idea. But after Simon mentioned feeling as though the investigation was being steered in a particular direction, she couldn't shake the thought from her head.

It was a feeling that intensified the second they arrested Felicity Horsfall and held up the evidence bag, which contained the gun in front of her face. The woman's eyes widened with genuine surprise as she babbled to them both about having no idea how the firearm had been found in her house. Not surprising, granted. Not many people would own up to having a gun in their house; it was a guaranteed prison sentence, after all, but Emma knew honesty when she saw it.

So, if Felicity Horsfall had nothing whatsoever to do with the gun, which early investigation seemed to support it being the gun which killed Winston Mayhew, then the only possible explanation for it being there was because it had been placed there by person, or persons, unknown.

Not that Emma thought for a second that Edith and Branwell had anything to do with it, but those two certainly seemed to have their finger on the pulse where the inhabitants of Hinklebury were concerned and, in fairness to the pair, their own secret investigation had come up trumps on several occasions.

Emma had left Simon back at the station, citing that she needed to run a quick errand while he compiled his list of questions he intended to quiz Felicity about in the interview room. And in many respects, she supposed that it was an errand of sorts. Maybe Edith and Branwell might offer helpful insight into Felicity; it certainly didn't hurt to ask.

But when she arrived, she spotted Edith and Branwell hurrying from her flat with furtive expressions, and the copper in Emma told her that they were up to something. She trailed them slowly, thanking the unknown gods above for her electric, practically noiseless car as she kerbed-crawled behind them.

She turned off the engine outside Winston Mayhew's home, shrunk in her seat, and peered at them through the steering wheel as they spoke to the constable outside the house. Although she couldn't hear a word, she could quite quickly tell that they were convincing the PC of something, coaxing him into whatever it was they were after. Sure enough, after a couple of minutes of persuasion, the constable moved out of the way and let them inside the house.

Unprofessional? Absolutely. A disciplinary offence for the constable? Undoubtedly. But Emma knew just how wearing Edith and Branwell could be, and she was certain that even she would hand over her bank card and PIN to them if they had the opportunity to work on her for long enough.

They were only inside for a matter of minutes, five at the most, and they emerged looking more confused than when they had entered. She watched them pass her on the other side of the road, heading toward the shops so deep in conversation that they didn't even see her sitting in the car.

She was going to pull up alongside them and reprimand them for being inside the murder victim's home. She also considered throwing in a guilt-trip comment about the lowly constable who would soon be out of a job thanks to their general busy-body behaviour. Still, something told Emma that the brother and sister duo weren't finished just yet.

Maybe she'd let them continue the escapade a little longer and see just how much the pair knew.

Chapter Twenty Eight

The village bank was a quiet one, which, unsurprisingly, was faced with the threat of closure thanks in no small part to the invention of online banking.

Maureen had been flicking through her copy of *Take a Break* with a cup of coffee in her hand when Edith and Branwell entered, which she quickly deposited out of sight beneath the counter as they approached the desk.

Just as Edith suspected, Maureen had been only too keen to divulge her recent interaction with DCI Jackman and DS Hooper the other day.

'I mean, if I'm being honest with you,' said Maureen quietly. 'In a small branch like this, we get to know everything about our customer's financial circumstances. And I mean everything.'

Everything? Edith made a mental note to close her account with the branch before her inheritance was deposited.

'We know how much gets paid in,' continued Maureen. 'We know where the money comes from, how much a person spends—where they spend it, even who their mobile phone provider is. Nothing gets past us. But the art of being a good bank teller is knowing when to keep things to yourself.'

'And so when it came to Harry Lanscombe, you always knew that he had a substantial balance in his account?' asked Branwell.

Maureen vigorously nodded her head. 'Absolutely. He came in and withdrew thirty pounds a week, every Monday morning, nine o'clock on the dot. Sometimes, he'd make a deposit on the same day, but it was never more than a couple of pounds in pennies and coppers. It was like he'd been delving down the back of the settee for them. But then, he made those huge deposits on three occasions, which had us all talking after he'd left.'

'When were these deposits made?' asked Edith.

Maureen leaned closer towards them, and Edith caught the unmistakable whiff of tuna lingering on her breath. In her opinion, tuna, onions, and garlic should be outlawed for anyone working with the public.

'The last one, the fifteen grand, that was only a couple of days before he was killed,' whispered Maureen.

'And the other deposits? The ones for five thousand and seven thousand?' asked Branwell.

'They were deposited around three months before he died,' a voice behind them said, causing the three co-conspirators to jump and turn around.

DS Emma Hooper's unimpressed face stared back at them.

'Sergeant,' said Branwell cheerily. 'How lovely to see you again.'

'I wish I could return the compliment,' Emma said sardonically. 'And does the branch manager know, Mrs O'Hara, just how helpful you are with customers? Even when the information you're giving is a complete breach of the Data Protection Act?'

Maureen's face paled. 'I don't know what you mean,' she exclaimed. 'Mrs Elliott and her brother were just asking me about the benefits of opening an ISA account.'

Emma folded her arms across her chest. 'Is this true?' she asked Edith and Branwell.

'Not even close,' admitted Branwell. 'Do I look like the kind of man who needs an ISA?'

'Come with me, please,' said Emma, heading towards the door. 'Oh, and Mrs O'Hara – discretion works both ways. I'll overlook your actions today, but I suggest you stop divulging personal information about the bank's customers in the future.'

Edith cast an apologetic glance at Maureen, who shook profusely as she returned to her seat, retrieved her copy of Take a Break, and pretended to read the pages without looking back up as they left. Edith felt a slight pang of guilt for Maureen, but then she remembered what she'd said about knowing everything about the customer's finances, and she baulked as she recalled that Sarah had once used her debit card to buy a slinky nightdress from Ann Summer's; she prayed that whoever might have spotted that transaction on her account didn't think that it was for her.

'Get in the car,' Emma instructed when they were back outside.

'Are we under arrest?' asked Branwell. 'Because unless we are, I politely decline your offer.'

Emma took a deep breath. 'Would you like me to arrest you? Because I certainly have grounds, seeing as I've just spotted you coming out of Winston Mayhew's house. And just now, obtaining private information from Maureen O'Hara about one of the victims.'

'Ah! But are they actually offences?' asked Branwell. 'In my mind, it was no more than popping around to a neighbour's house and then having a friendly chat with another about the village's ongoing murderous crisis.'

'In my mind, it's called tampering with evidence, withholding evidence, and possibly perverting the course of justice. Now get in,' Emma said sternly, unlocking the car doors.

'Clunk, click, every trip,' said Branwell as he pulled his seatbelt across his chest and fastened it. 'I don't want you throwing in a charge of not wearing a seatbelt to your ever-growing list of offences.'

'Are you taking us to the station again?' asked Edith as Emma put the car into gear and drove off. 'I don't think I'll be able to hold my head up again in the village if I step foot in there for a third time.'

But to Edith's surprise, Emma shook her head. 'You can hold your head up for another day, Mrs Elliott. I'm taking you home.'

When they returned to Edith's flat, they congregated in the living room. Edith perched herself nervously on the edge of the armchair cushion while Branwell made them all drinks.

'Can I ask what this is all about?' she asked Emma, who was busy staring at Edith's photographs hanging on the walls.

'Felicity Horsfall,' she said, turning to face Edith. 'What do you think about her?'

'Felicity? I wouldn't say I know her that well,' she replied with a shrug, and Edith spotted the slight sag in Emma's shoulders. 'But,' she continued, 'I'd say from what we've discovered, she definitely had more dealings with Harry Lanscombe than she's letting on.'

'In what way,' urged Emma.

'I think she's in trouble financially speaking,' said Edith, as Branwell entered the living room with three glasses of Pimm's which Edith had no idea where he'd got from.

'She's offering ludicrous deals in the café,' he said as he handed Emma a glass. 'It just screams desperation. And she became extremely defensive when we were questioning...I mean, *asking* her about having some form of dealings with Harry. She was practically all over me up until that point.'

'She denied it, of course,' added Edith. 'Which we know to be a lie because the photographs of her outside his house proved otherwise. So the question then becomes, why is she lying?'

'Indeed,' said Emma. 'A question that will be put to her when she's questioned later this morning.'

Branwell stopped drinking from his glass. 'She's in custody? On what charge?'

'Murder,' said Emma bluntly. 'And possession of a firearm.'

A small gasp escaped Edith's lips. 'A firearm? Is it the same one that was used to kill Winston?'

Emma nodded. 'It appears so, but that's still to be confirmed.'

Edith sat back in the chair, and her eyes stared off into a trance. After a few seconds, she sat up again. 'How did you know about the gun? What made you search her house?'

'Tip-off – anonymous before you ask. And no, we have no idea who the mystery caller was. It was made from an unregistered pay-as-you-go phone.'

'Humm,' said Edith, sitting back down in the chair. 'And how did Felicity react when you presented her with the evidence?'

Emma set down the drink, which hardly surprised Edith, seeing as she was on duty. 'Flabbergasted, if I'm being honest. Simon, that is, DCI Jackman, believes that something isn't quite right with how we're coming by information, and I tend to agree with him, especially after this morning. That woman had never seen that gun before in her life, so if that's the case...'

'Then who put it there,' finished Edith.

'Exactly,' agreed Emma.

Branwell polished off the remnants of his glass and, seeing that Emma had no intention of drinking hers, picked up her glass and proceeded to drink. 'Why did you come here to talk to us about it?' he asked.

Emma sat on the little sofa, placed her hands on her knees and sighed. 'Have you ever felt that somebody is always one step ahead of you?'

'Story of my life,' joked Branwell.

'Well, that's how I feel about you two,' she continued, ignoring his little quip. 'I think you're better positioned to wheedle out bits of information than we are. It's as though you already have all the bits of the jigsaw, and you just need to put all the pieces together to get the full picture.'

'So you thought it would be a good idea to join forces? How thrilling!' said Branwell.

'I'd prefer to call it pooling resources,' said Emma.

'We should have a name for our little amalgamation,' he said, not listening to her. 'Crime busters? Who you gonna call and all that...'

'No. Absolutely not,' replied Emma.

The Old Bill? We're obviously the old element in the double act, and you and DCI Jackman are...'

'Jesus! No, Branwell,' Emma replied sternly.

Crimewatch? No, wait. That's an old television programme, isn't it? How about Crimewatchers instead?

Emma looked Edith square in the eyes. 'Actually, I think I will have that glass of Pimm's.'

Chapter Twenty Nine

Simon looked up at the station wall clock and frowned. Where the hell was Emma this time? She said she'd only be half an hour, but it had been almost two. Didn't she realise that they had a suspect to interview? Of course, she realised it in the same way she knew that they only had twenty-four hours to hold a suspect. If she didn't come back soon, then Simon would have to conduct the interview with Felicity on his own. Five more minutes – that's all he'd give her, and then that was it.

He returned to his desk and pulled open the drawer; he'd need sustenance to see him through the rest of the day. Simon's sneaky little stash consisted of a Toffee Crisp, a large bag of Doritos, and a chocolate muffin pumped full of nasty preservatives that the sell-by date was a year in advance. Not the most hearty of meals, he admitted, but it'd give him the temporary sugar rush that his body was craving at that moment.

But as if on cue, Emma hurried breathlessly through the door to the office, and he quickly pushed the door closed again. Did she have a secret camera somewhere watching his every move?

'I'm sorry,' she said, whipping off her coat and draping it on the back of her chair. 'It took longer than I thought.'

'Where were you?' asked Simon, unable to conceal his frustration. 'Two bloody hours, Em.'

'I know, I know,' she said, holding her hands up in defence. 'I'll tell you about it later. Have you interviewed her yet?'

Simon shook his head. 'I was just about to. Are you joining me? Or can't you spare the time?'

Emma's eyes narrowed. 'Okay, moody arse. Don't take it out on me because you haven't had your daily fix.'

Simon did his best to adopt a confused expression, but it was lost somewhere between the fear of Emma, yet again, hitting the nail on the head and the expression landing on his face.

'Enough,' he told her as he picked up his notepad. 'Let's get it over with.'

They walked out of the office to head down to the cells where Felicity had been languishing for most of the morning, and on his way out, he cast a cautious glance around his desk to see if Emma had indeed hidden a spy camera somewhere among his things.

'So, you're denying all knowledge of the gun?' Simon asked Felicity.

Felicity's solicitor whispered something in her ear, and she tutted. 'No. I'm not saying no comment to everything,' she reprimanded him. 'I haven't done anything wrong. That's right – I have never seen the wretched thing in my life.'

'That's convenient,' said Emma, earning her a hateful stare from Felicity. 'So, how do you believe it got there?'

'Quite obviously, someone must have put it there,' she replied sardonically.

Simon picked up his pen and poised it over his notepad. 'And who might that be? Do you have any names?'

Felicity stared into space and sighed heavily as she ran a hand through her hair. 'I've had so many visitors since this whole thing started. You know what people can be like; they claim to be checking that you're okay, but in reality, they're only coming around because they're being nosey.

But I won't believe that any of them would have done something like that to me.'

'Clearly, somebody in your village is a murderer, and if the gun found stashed behind your rather interesting selection of DVDs wasn't put there by you as you claim it wasn't, then it stands to reason that it must have been one of your visitors,' said Simon.

Felicity's face darkened. 'What I watch in the privacy of my own home is entirely up to me. So, don't get snooty with me, young man.'

'Let's park the raunchy DVDs and the gun's location to one side for a moment,' interrupted Emma. 'I want to ask you about something else.'

Simon looked down at his notepad—this wasn't part of his organised list of questions. What did Emma think she was doing deviating from his plan?

'We have in our possession a photograph of your standing outside Harry's home, which was taken, we believe, a week or so before his death. And yet, in previous questioning, you denied having anything to do with the man. Can you explain that?' asked Emma as she leaned back in the chair and folded her arms.

Felicity's eyes widened, exposing the blood-shot whites. She momentarily held her gaze on Emma, looked at her solicitor and then back at Emma.

'No comment,' she said bluntly.

'And now you want to go no comment? When only seconds ago, you were all too keen to talk, seeing as you were innocent? There's no point trying clamming up now; we'll get to the bottom of it all eventually,' pressed Emma.

Simon viewed the woman opposite him carefully, spotting the conflicting stages of emotion manifesting on her face: She was on the verge of breaking down; he could sense it! Good job, Emma, he thought to himself. However, he'd have to have a word with her later about taking over in the interview room.

Felicity rested her elbows on the table, planted her head in her hands, and began to sob uncontrollably. Yes! Although, he probably shouldn't get too excited about making an elderly lady cry. If somebody had done that to his mother, he probably would have punched them straight on the end of their nose – DCI or not.

He and Emma remained silent, keeping any compassion under wraps and allowing Felicity the time to realise that the game was well and truly up. But what game, exactly, remained to be seen? Finally, she lifted her head and sniffed back the clear liquid oozing from her nostrils.

'He said it was a sound investment,' she blubbed. 'He made out that it was a minimal risk, and I'd have a fifty percent return on my money – fifty percent!'

'What investment?' said Emma, whose tone had surprisingly softened. 'Tell us exactly what happened between you and Harry.'

Felicity wiped the tears from her cheeks with the back of her hand and cleared her throat. 'I was in such a mess, you see. The rent for the café had increased, and we're not talking about a few quid; it was over four thousand pounds a year more to extend the lease. I'd been struggling with the bills for a while, but with that type of hike in my outgoings, I knew there was no way I'd be able to meet the payments. People aren't prepared to spend like they used to. Everything is so much tighter for everybody financially since COVID.'

'And Harry told you about some scheme with a good return, I take it?' said Simon.

Felicity nodded again. 'Yes. He said that nothing could go wrong; some environmental investment to do with renewable energy. Well, that sort of thing seems all the rage nowadays, doesn't it? He'd mentioned it in passing one of the days that he came into the café. He didn't push me or anything like that; he just mentioned it in general conversation, ate his cake, drank his coffee, and then left. After he'd gone, I couldn't get it out of my mind. I mean, if I could make that kind of money, I wouldn't have to worry about the bills for the next couple of years. So, when he came back in a few days later, I asked him about it.'

'How much did you give him?' asked Emma.

Felicity took a deep breath. 'Everything I had – fifteen thousand pounds.'

'And this was the week of his death?' asked Simon.

'Yes, a few days before,' said Felicity.

'Did you transfer the money to him, or did you give it to him in cash?' he continued.

'Cash. He said it was a limited entry market, so there weren't many spaces for investors. If I gave the money to him in cash, he'd sort it all out under his name, and when it came to fruition, we'd divvy up the return. So, I gave it to him – just like that! But in my head, I didn't sense any danger. I'd known Harry for years, and he didn't seem the type to take advantage of anybody like that.'

'When did you realise that something was wrong?' asked Simon.

Now, they were getting to the nitty gritty of it all. Poor old Harry Lanscombe wasn't the innocent pensioner he appeared to be; he was nothing more than a common scam artist.

'Literally, the next day. I'd gone to his house to talk to him and see if he'd made the investment. But he wouldn't answer the door to me, and I knew that he was in because

I'd seen him go inside. And he never came back to the café or answered my phone calls, and my heart just sank to the depths of my stomach.'

Simon pushed his notepad to the side of the table and leaned closer to Felicity. 'When did you see him again?' he asked.

'At the cricket match. I was at the cake stand, and he was sitting at the bar, drowning his sorrows because he'd already fluffed the game. I went over to him and asked him what was going on. He just looked up at me with this stupid smug grin spreading across his face, and I asked him what he was smiling about.'

'And what was his response?' asked Emma.

A fresh round of tears trickled out of Felicity's eyes. 'He looked me dead in the eyes and said, what money? I have no idea what you're talking about. And I said to him, don't be silly, Harry. I can prove that I gave you the fifteen grand, and he scoffed at me and said, really? What proof? Did you do a bank transfer? No. Did you get an agreement in writing between us? No. He was so uncaring and unfeeling – not like the Harry I'd been talking to. No fool like an old fool. I suppose I deserved everything that I got.'

Emma reached into her pocket, pulled out a packet of tissues, and slid them across the table to Felicity.

'You shouldn't feel bad about it. We think you're not the first person Mr Lanscombe has done this to. The man was a con artist,' said Emma, her voice heavy with sympathy as she reached over and took Felicity's hand in hers, surprising Simon yet again. 'You should have come to us and reported him for fraud and obtaining money by deception.'

'But like Harry said, I had no proof. How long would something like that take? Months? Years? By then, my money would have been long gone – it might already be gone. Lord knows what he's done with it. And the village would have known what a stupid old woman I'd been. I just couldn't live with the humiliation,' said Felicity.

Simon softened. 'We think Harry deposited your money into his personal bank account, and it's still very much there. At the end of the investigation, we can assist you with recovering it, provided everything you say checks out. It won't be a quick process, but at least you know it's not gone forever.' He looked up at the clock. 'I think we'll leave it there and terminate the interview, but before I do, would you be able to give us that list of names of visitors to your home?'

'One more question before you do that,' Emma interrupted again, and Simon suppressed the urge to pull rank. 'So that we're all clear – did you kill Harry Lanscombe?'

Felicity stared back at them and the earlier sorrow in her face ebbed away. 'No,' she replied bluntly. 'But I wish to God I had.'

Chapter Thirty

T he Bentley sped around the corner, sending a spray of pebbles and dust in its wake.

'For the love of God, Branwell, will you slow down?' Edith pleaded as she gripped the door handle.

Branwell, in response, pressed his foot down on the accelerator.

'Absolutely not, Edie,' he replied as he whizzed along the road even faster. 'If I go any slower, you'll seize your opportunity and jump out of the car.'

To be fair to her brother, he was right. When Branwell had first suggested that they go out for a leisurely drive to clear their heads, she'd been all too ready to jump into the passenger seat and fasten her seatbelt. Village life had suddenly become stifling for Edith; two murders might not have seemed like a lot by a larger city's standard, but for the small population of Hinklebury, it was two murders too many. Everywhere Edith looked, she saw suspects, not neighbours, under her investigative glare. As much as it pained her to think that way, one person amongst them was a cold-blooded killer, and until she discovered who that person was, she knew that she'd never be able to relax again fully.

Edith breathed deeply, inhaling the air whooshing in through the open car window. Branwell had promised her a special treat.

'Somewhere where you can be you again,' he'd told her as he put the car into gear and navigated his way out of the village.

But as the journey progressed, Edith spotted familiar road signs, and her heartbeat picked up its pace.

'Where are we going exactly?' she asked him.

His eyes darted in her direction for a second before fixing themselves back on the road again. He was nervous, and Branwell was never nervous, citing that nerves were for people who had no belief in their own convictions. But seeing his knuckles whiten as his fingers tightened around the steering wheel filled her whole body with dread.

'You'll thank me later,' he told her. 'We knew it had to happen at some point, so I thought I'd take the initiative and get it over and done with.'

The memories she'd buried deep in her mind came flooding back, triggered by each road sign, rolling hillsides, and even the trees lining the roads. Why was Branwell doing this to her?

'Stop the car now,' she insisted, but Branwell drove faster.

'It'll be over in a jiffy,' he said as he turned the car sharply on the following corner and sped through a set of wrought iron gates.

The driveway to the house was as ridiculously long as Edith remembered, where a building in the distance seemed impossibly tiny but grew in size with each revolution of the car wheels until there, in all of its imposing glory, was Althorp Hall.

Branwell pulled up alongside the house, turned off the engine and faced her in his seat. In her peripheral vision, she saw a flurry of movement, and she knew without turning that the household staff were coming outside to greet the master of the house and his guest.

'We're here now,' Branwell told her. 'May as well get out and see how the old girl is faring these days.'

The doors clunked unlocked, and Edith's door was opened from the outside.

'Mrs Elliott,' said an unfamiliar voice. 'We've been expecting you. Welcome home.'

Home. This hadn't been Edith's home for fifty years, but as she reluctantly got out of the car, she was hit with the striking beauty of the hall; it felt as though she'd only been away for a few weeks.

Everything was the same as it always had been: a building frozen in time while the world around it had moved on. The brickwork still had the same weathered façade; the windows gleamed, the ivy trailing up the side of the house remained.

Edith's gaze drifted down to the staff standing in a line and beaming back at her with expectant faces. Should she say something? It felt like she should judging by how they were looking at her, but this was hardly a royal visit.

Branwell slid up beside her and held out his arm. 'Shall we, sister dearest?' he said. 'Crosby, would you bring some drinks into the drawing-room?'

Crosby, the butler, stepped forward and bowed his head. It seemed that even those traditions remained, too, no matter how archaic they were now.

'Of course, Sir. What would you like?'

'The usual for me,' said Branwell. 'And neat vodka for my sister; she drinks like a fish.'

Edith nudged him in the ribs. 'A sweet tea would be lovely, thank you, Crosby.'

Branwell led Edith up the stone steps and through the enormous front door, transporting her back to a life she thought she'd never see again.

'How has it been?' Branwell asked her later that afternoon. 'As bad as you thought it would be?'

Edith shook her head. In truth, she'd never felt more at ease. She could never imagine living at Althorp Hall again, but she couldn't deny that something buried in her chromosomes gave her a sense of belonging.

'It's been a journey of discovery,' she replied.

'Ah! A discovery of what, though? That's the question.'

She sat on the pink velvet sofa and sank into the down cushions. Like much of the furniture in the hall, it was in remarkably good condition, given its age. Branwell had done a remarkable job keeping everything in order, which, considering this was Branwell she was talking about, was quite a surprise: She'd half expected him to turn the place into a casino and lap dancing club, in all honesty.

Edith played with the fringe tassels that lined the cushions and shrugged. 'Of being reminded of who I am deep down and reinforcing my belief that who I became because of leaving here was the right thing to do.'

'Very profound,' replied Branwell. 'So, you wouldn't consider moving back here? It'd be nice to have some company again.'

'Oh Lord, no,' replied Edith, chuckling. 'I'd feel isolated all of the way out here. There's no other house around for miles. It's alright for you; you drive, and you flit off somewhere without a moment's notice. I'd feel like I was slowly being suffocated if I lived here. I much prefer being where I am, in my little friendly community, where there's always somebody on hand if you need them.'

'And obviously, there's your friendly neighbourhood murderer as well,' he replied sarcastically. 'Who wouldn't want to live somewhere where the possibility of being bumped off by a homicidal manic was a real one.'

'And yet, you've elected to stay at mine these past few days,' replied Edith. 'Admit it, you love it there too.'

He gave a sly grin. 'I'm only staying to make sure you're safe, Edie. Not for any other reason.'

'Fibber,' she shot back at him, and Branwell gave her a quick wink.

'Anyway, on the cheery topic of homicidal murderers, how goes your super-sleuth brain? Have you made sense of it all yet?'

'It's like Emma said. It's all here,' she replied, tapping the side of her head. 'I just need to slot everything into place. But for whatever reason, it's not coming together.'

'It's probably the booze,' replied Branwell. 'You are drinking quite a lot lately.'

'Pot, kettle, black, springs to mind,' she told Branwell.

'But this kettle certainly doesn't need any polishing,' he shot back.

Edith's mobile phone pinged with a notification, and she retrieved it from her handbag.

'Talk of the devil. It's Emma. She's asked to meet with us again. What shall I tell her?'

'Oh goody,' replied Branwell, downing the rest of his drink. 'Get your things together, and let's head back to yours. The Crimewatchers are in business!'

Chapter Thirty One

Simon resumed his position in front of the fireplace in Edith's flat and stared around the living room at the other occupants. How had Emma talked him into this? In his opinion, it was not just ridiculous but completely unprofessional, akin to consulting a medium for help. He was all for working with members of the public, but consulting them as though they were fellow officers of the law was ludicrous.

When he and Emma first exited the interview room after their rather enlightening discussion with Felicity Horsfall, he opened his mouth to protest her interference, even if it did yield amazing results; it just didn't do to be undermined in front of suspects. But Emma had quickly shushed him, much to his surprise and annoyance, and pulled him into a vacant interview room.

'I need to tell you something,' she said in hushed tones. 'Just don't be mad at me.'

That last time she'd used that sentence, it was to tell Simon that she'd accidentally dropped his mobile phone down a drain when he'd asked her to hold it while he tied his shoelace; a simple enough mistake, but it had enraged Simon nonetheless – she'd only had it in her hands for less than thirty seconds.

'Go on,' he urged, making no promises at all.

Emma had gone into a generous and, to his trained ears, well-rehearsed speech about how she'd spoken about the case to Edith and Branwell. How she felt they were further along than they were, and if somebody was nudging them in this direction and that, then who better positioned to discover who that person was? After all, they lived amongst this unknown assailant, probably knew them personally, and if that were the case, then surely it made sense to have them onside? If Edith and Branwell thought that they were working personally on the case, then didn't it make it more likely for them to forward any information they discovered rather than keep it to themselves?

Simon had never wanted to immediately sack somebody on the spot as much as he did at that moment. He wasn't sure whether it was the widening of his eyes at Emma's revelation or the shocking red his face went as the fury crept onto his cheeks that made Emma grab his arm.

'Please, Simon...Sir. Will you just trust me on this one? I've never let you down before, and I don't intend to start now,' she pleaded.

Simon let out a heavy sigh and rubbed his face with his hands. 'Is there anything else I need to know?' he asked her. 'Have you organised them to have warrant cards? Got them a uniform sorted? Issued them was a taser gun?'

Emma shook her head. 'No, nothing like that. But I should warn you that Branwell is thinking up names for our new little alliance.'

'Oh Jesus,' Simon whispered under his breath.

And now, here he was, in the most unorthodox situation in all of his career, unless you counted that rather unfortunate incident with the farmer who got rather amorous with one of his cows, but the less said about that, the better.

Edith once again sat next to Emma on the small sofa, looking sheepishly up at him, knowing full well that Simon was on the verge of arresting them all. Branwell, by contrast, having not noticed the tension in the air, harped on about getting special badges made for them all.

'No name badges,' Simon told him firmly. 'This is absolutely a one-off, so let's not get carried away. DS Hooper has explained the circumstances to me, and I'm inclined to agree, although extremely reluctantly, that there may be some benefit in...' In what exactly, he thought to himself. Working together? Pooling resources? Those words felt unnatural to him. 'hearing what you have to say,' he said finally. Yes. That sounded about right.

Edith looked up at him. 'There's something terribly wrong here, Inspector,' she said, her eyes narrowing.

'You tend to get that feeling when people are being murdered,' he said sarcastically.

'But it's more than that. There's an element of such devious pre-meditation at play,' she said to him.

'I have to be honest, I was hoping for something a little more insightful than that,' Simon told her.

'Go on, Edie. Tell him,' urged Branwell. 'He thinks we're a couple or morons clutching at straws.'

'I don't think you're morons,' interjected Simon.

'But you do think we're clutching straws?' asked Branwell.

Simon rolled his eyes and looked back at Edith. 'Mrs Elliott. I'd be grateful if you could share any thoughts on the murders.'

He noted the brief crinkle in the corners of her eyes and the millisecond of smile that flashed on her lips, pleased at being asked for her opinion. She took a deep breath, and Simon braced himself; please, God, don't let this be a waste of time; otherwise, he'd be lumbered with them for the remainder of the investigation.

'If we ignore the fact that somebody is deliberately trying to guide this investigation and look at what we know, let's start with the victims. Neither of them was entirely innocent. But I think that Harry was always the intended target. His bank balance would suggest he syphoned money from whoever could.'

Simon's eyes darted to Emma.

'I didn't show them Mr Lanscombe's bank account,' she protested. 'Blame the O'Hara woman who works in the bank.'

'There were three large deposits, one of which, the latest, being accounted for by Felicity Horsfall. But the other two deposits? The owner or owners of that money is yet to be determined. So, if Harry had a penchant for defrauding people, then it's likely that one of those people, realising that they weren't about to get their money back any time soon, decided to deliver their own justice.'

'Agreed,' said Simon.

'So, that person must have known that Harry had taken money from Felicity too because why would they hide the gun in her home?'

'Lucky guess?' said Emma.

'I don't think it was,' continued Edith. 'I think that the murderer spotted what Harry was doing to Felicity and recognised the signs. I think that they took advantage of the fact and always meant for Felicity to be arrested and charged with his murder. As for poor Winston, he was just in the wrong place, at the wrong time.'

'With a camera,' added Branwell.

'And it's the camera that got him killed,' said Edith, keeping her gaze fixed on Simon. 'Or, more specifically, the photographs. I saw him at the cricket match, and yet, instead of admitting it, he lied to you and said he wasn't. And the reason he lied was because he saw the murderer going behind the marquee on the day and probably emerging again after they'd killed Harry.'

'It's plausible,' agreed Simon. He perched himself on the arm of the sofa next to Edith and looked down at her. 'But why keep quiet about it? He would have instantly known who killed Harry, so why not tell us?'

'Because, knowing Winston as I did, he was a lonely man looking for love or companionship, just anything that would mean he wasn't alone anymore. He came here once, just after Ronnie died, with an awful casserole. I could see what he was up to immediately.'

'Never trust a man who cooks casseroles,' said Branwell.

'So, he was planning to do what exactly? Blackmail the murderer to be his friend?' said Emma. 'That sounds a little far-fetched, don't you think?'

'Loneliness makes us do very strange things,' said Edith.

Her eyes flicked to the fireplace, and Simon turned, following her gaze. Seeing only an urn and a couple of framed photographs, he turned back to face her.

'So, Winston approached the murderer, and he had to die too because of what he knew,' continued Edith. 'I don't think that he was ever part of the plan. This has always been about Harry.'

'Any ideas who this mastermind is?' asked Simon.

'Let's look at the suspects,' said Edith. 'Brian and Sally Marston to start. We know that Brian had fallen out with Harry when Harry tried to get a discount on his meal in the pub that lunchtime. And we also know that Winston had taken some rather provocative photographs of them in their bedroom. Then Felicity Horsfall, of course. She may be denying all knowledge of the gun, but Harry did defraud her out of a considerable sum of money, and once again, Winston had an incriminating photograph of her outside Harry's house, and let's not forget she was the one to find the body.'

'Brian Marston had the opportunity to commit both of the murders,' said Simon. 'He was in the marquee serving beer at the time of Harry's murder. He could have just slipped out of the back panel, killed Harry and slipped back in again unseen. And he's already admitted to having gone to Winston's house the night he was killed while his wife was in the bath. Just because he says Winston was already dead when he got there doesn't mean he's telling the truth.'

'But if that's the case, then he had to have accessed Felicity's house to plant the gun,' said Edith.

Simon reached into his pocket and retrieved the folded piece of paper. He opened it and scanned the list of names Felicity had written for him.

'Then it couldn't have been him because neither he nor Sally visited Felicity's house at all since Harry or Winston were murdered,' he said to them.

'Which leaves Felicity,' said Edith. 'But yet, I don't believe that having had her money stolen less than a week prior, her first reaction would be to kill Harry.'

'A couple of months later, perhaps,' agreed Branwell. 'But not a week. Not when there was a chance she could be wrong, and she could still get her money back from Harry.'

Simon reached forward and dropped the list on the coffee table. 'So, that leaves us no better off than we were before. We still don't know who killed them,' he said as his face crumpled with frustration.

Edith leaned forward and, with a gentle shake of her head, picked up the list. 'Not at all, Inspector. Because one of the names on this list killed Harry and Winston. It has to be one of them because they had access to Felicity's house to plant the gun.' Her eyes drifted down the page. 'For a start, we should discount the men because these murders definitely have a woman's touch about them. Harry could easily swindle money out of a woman, but a man? And Winston wouldn't be interested in male companionship.' Her eyes suddenly stopped, settling on something on the list, and she let her hand drop into her lap as she stared in disbelief at nothing in particular on the wall in front of her.

'Edith?' asked Simon. 'Are you okay?'

'Crumbs. I've seen that look before. I think we've lost her,' joked Branwell, and Edith turned her head sharply to face him.

'What did you just say?' she asked him.

'I said I've seen that look before...'

'No,' interrupted Edith. 'Not that bit.' And then looking up at Simon, she said, 'I think we need to speak to

Damien Lanscombe again, and Branwell, I think it's about time we went and picked up those photographs from the developers.'

Simon looked at Emma. 'What photographs,' he mouthed at her, and Emma shrugged her shoulders.

'We need to check those now because if I'm right, then I know who murdered Harry and Winston,' said Edith.

Chapter Thirty Two

They were all sitting inside Felicity's café: Brian and Sally Marston, Felicity Horsfall, Edith, Branwell, and, of course, Emma and Simon. When Edith first suggested that they gather all of the suspects in one place, she spotted Simon's repressed eye roll, but it was something that Edith had longed to do for her entire life and after a bit of cajoling from her and Branwell, he'd reluctantly agreed. Even Emma had sided with her, citing that, seeing as Edith had unravelled the whole mystery, it was only fair that he agreed.

Branwell, never one to miss an opportunity to expand his waistline, was tucking into a hearty slice of carrot cake provided by a nervous Felicity, who had been released earlier that day and quite publicly dropped back home in the back of a police car, much to the shock and surprise of the village. A small crowd of gawkers had gathered outside the window of the café, nudging each other out of the way as they vied for the best viewing spot despite having no idea what was happening.

The door jingled, and in bustled Sarah, her face filled with concern as she rushed to Edith's table.

'Edith!' she said breathlessly. 'What on earth is going on? It's all around the village that Felicity has been released. You shouldn't be here. That woman is capable of anything. Just because the police haven't proven it yet doesn't make her innocent.'

'I agree,' Brian piped up. 'There's no smoke without fire.'

'Sit down, Sarah, and I'll explain,' said Edith as she pulled out a chair for her friend. 'And Brian, I would have thought you'd be the last person to accuse somebody, given that you equally have a strong motive to want both men dead.'

Brian went to protest but quickly closed his mouth again.

'Don't speak to my husband like that,' interjected Sally. 'He's right. We all know it was her.' She jabbed a finger in Felicity's direction. 'I watch *Law and Order* – the evidence is never wrong.'

'Why don't you watch what you say? We all know what you and your husband get up to, you filthy deviants,' Felicity spat back.

'There'll be tarts flying all over the place in a minute, and I'm not talking about the pastries,' Branwell whispered in Edith's ear.

Sally jumped up from her chair and bounded towards Felicity, who shrank back behind Simon's back.

'Sit down, Mrs Marston, unless you want to be arrested for aggravated assault,' Emma said, gripping the woman's arm and guiding her back to her chair.

'The evidence is there because somebody put it there for us to find,' said Edith, unconcerned by the imminent catfight. 'Somebody infiltrated this investigation from the very beginning, quite cleverly so, if I might add. But unfortunately, for them at least, their meddling is what's led us to discover who they are.'

She left a deliberate pause, leaving her words lingering in the air. Edith was loving every second of this.

'Well, go on then, woman. Who was it?' demanded Brian.

'In order for us to make sense of everything, we have to go back to the beginning,' continued Edith, ignoring him. 'Harry, as we now know, accumulated much of his wealth from defrauding people. He even stole from his own son, which fractured their relationship completely, and he went to great lengths to hide away in a sleepy village to see out the rest of his days in peace. But the lure of money was too much for Harry, and with so many lonely women to prey on, he couldn't help himself. Felicity admitted that Harry stole fifteen thousand pounds from her, which accounted for the latest deposit into his account, but what about the other two deposits made months before?'

'What about them?' asked Sarah. 'What's so important about those?'

Edith turned to her friend, sorrow creeping into her eyes. 'Oh, Sarah. Why didn't you tell me?'

Sarah let out a small scoff. 'Tell you what, Edith? You're confusing me now.'

'That you gave Harry money too. It needn't have come to murder. I would have helped you get it back.'

Sarah stood sharply. 'Me? I didn't kill Harry. It was her,' she pointed at Felicity. 'Or what about his son? What's his name, Damien? I saw him outside Harry's house shouting through the letterbox.'

Simon placed a firm hand on Sarah's shoulder. 'Sit down please, Mrs Winslow,' he said, pushing her back into her seat.

'You couldn't have seen Damien Lanscombe outside his father's house. He lives in Hong Kong,' said Edith.

'And that, ultimately, was your downfall. You described Harry's son to a tee, right down to his purple mohawk hair, but we had a conversation with Damien earlier today, a video call, and his hair is a greying crew cut. He got rid of the mohawk in the mid-nineties, not long after he and has father became estranged. And the only way you could have known about that haircut was from the old photograph that Harry had of them both in his home. You must have been inside at some point, probably when Harry was trying to schmooze you for money. And when Harry got the money and cut you off, a kernel of an idea sprouted in your mind.'

Sarah shuffled in her chair. 'Edith. You're talking utter nonsense.'

'You decided to kill Harry and frame somebody else – it didn't matter who, just as long as it wasn't you. You even insinuated I might have something to do with it following the accident at the cricket pitch because it was you who DC Aaron Phillips remembers telling him that there was an unresolved animosity between Harry and me. It was you who lied and said that it was Harry's son outside his house when there was no way he could have been. It was you who went over to Felicity's house to plant the gun, and it was you who then went on to contact the police to inform them it was there; I'm sure when the police search your possessions, they'll discover the pay-as-you-go phone that was used to make the call.'

Sarah's face blanched and she gripped her handbag close to her body.

'You killed Harry because he stole thousands of pounds from you. I thought it was odd when you complained about not getting the cake stand at the cricket match that day – you even mentioned being unable to pay your rent, even though you laughed it off afterwards. I don't think you intended to kill him that day in particular, but when you saw him sneak behind the marquee, you couldn't stop yourself from following him. You left the line for the toilet, picked up a spare cricket ball, went behind the marquee and hit him stone-cold dead.'

The café's atmosphere was electric, but Edith took no pleasure in it. This was her friend, one of her closest friends for many years. She thought she knew the woman inside and out; they'd always been there for each other, but not this time. Edith couldn't overlook murder—not even for her best friend.

'You thought you'd done enough to cast doubt onto other suspects. Poor Felicity. You knew what Harry was up to with her. You'd probably seen him through the window smooth-talking her and recognised the same tactics he'd used on you, and sadly, you didn't give two hoots about framing her – she was your rival after all, in cakes at least. But something went dreadfully wrong, and Winston had spotted you, and he told you, didn't he? Silly, naïve Winston told you everything he'd seen. When was that exactly?'

Sarah's eyes filled with tears. 'The night I came to yours, and we had cake. I left early because I had a documentary to watch,' she replied.

'Oh yes,' said Branwell. 'The orangutans.'

'He was outside the door as I was leaving. He'd come to speak to you about something, and he told me straight to my face what he'd seen. He wasn't unkind or judgmental, but he did make it clear that he wanted something from me in return. And the thought of it sickened me to my stomach. I just couldn't...and then I worried that if I told him no, what he might do – who he might tell if I turned him down. So, I arranged to go around to his house. I took the other half of the cake I'd brought to yours. And while he was eating it, I told him I needed the toilet. I knew he had his old service revolver; he'd bragged about it often enough. And it was just a matter of finding it, and then, well, that was that.'

Edith nodded slowly. 'Branwell found what he thought was sand around Winston's armchair. He thought it was sand, but it was only this afternoon that I realised it was cake crumbs. And then again, when we broke into Harry's flat...'

'Wait – you broke into Harry Lanscombe's?' interrupted Simon.

'Sorry, old chap. It was all for the greater good of the case,' replied Branwell.

'There were crumbs on his trousers where he had sat on a chair at Harry's. Then I remembered in the hospital when you visited when you sprayed your cake crumbs all over me as you spoke. It was a silly little detail, but it was enough to make me realise you were involved.'

'You are a bit of a messy monkey,' agreed Branwell.

'But just in case there was any doubt, Branwell managed to retrieve a certain number of undeveloped films from Winston's house,' continued Edith.

Simon glared at Branwell, who put up his hands in defence and mouthed sorry back at the inspector.

'Winston had his camera with him on the day of the cricket match and took lots of photographs,' said Edith, opening her handbag and pulling out a pile of photographs. She spread them out on the table, and everybody in the café surrounded her and peered over. It was like a chronological visual record of the murder of Harry Lanscombe: Harry going around to the back of the marquee, Sarah standing in the queue for the toilet, her head fixed in Harry's direction, Sarah leaving the queue, her crouching down by the side of the marquee picking up a cricket ball, disappearing behind the marquee, and then returning around the front, her face contorted with rage.

Edith looked up at Sarah, who was still staring at the photographs, unable to meet her gaze.

'I'm so sorry, Sarah,' said Edith, reaching for her friend's hand, but Sarah quickly pulled it away and dropped it in her lap.

'Mrs Winslow,' said Simon, stepping forward. 'Could you come with me, please.'

Sarah stood up without saying a word and allowed Simon, flanked by Emma, to lead her out of the café, past the shocked faces of those waiting outside, and straight into the waiting police car.

Edith felt her own tears burning behind her eyes and Branwell placed a tender hand on hers.

'Good show, old girl. Good show,' he told her.

Chapter Thirty Three

Anthony Morgan rechecked the paperwork and smiled back up at Edith.

'You missed that signature there,' he said, pushing the document across the desk towards her.

'Silly me,' said Edith, picking up the pen and scribbling her signature in the space. 'There. All done.'

Anthony took it back from her and rechecked it. 'Wonderful, Mrs Elliott. May I be the first to congratulate you on the purchase of your new home.'

It had been six months since Winston's death, but finally, probate had been granted, and his house went up for sale. Edith had already trawled all of the local estate agents, informing them that if they notified her immediately of when the property came on the market, she would make a very generous and very personal payment by way of a thank you. So, it was no surprise that her mobile started shrilling into life eight weeks ago as the agents battled to claim their reward. With the signatures in place, Winston's cottage was now hers; Dickens, in his own doggy way, would be thrilled.

'So, completion should occur in the next few days, but I'll liaise with the seller's solicitors to confirm. Was there anything else I can help you with?'

'Did you change my bank account details as I requested,' asked Edith.

She'd been perturbed by what Maureen O'Hara had told her at the bank. As much as she loved Hinklebury, she didn't want people to know about her wealth. It would only result in an onslaught of sob stories and tales of woe from people who, up until that point, had never really bothered with her before.

Branwell told her to man up and to put anybody who tried their luck firmly in their place.

'Show it off! I'd buy a bloody helicopter and park it on the village green if I were you,' he'd joked to her one night after staying over at the flat again.

Thank God for the spare bedrooms in Winston's house, or, to be factually correct, her house. She was aching in all manner of places on her body that she didn't even know existed, thanks to twisting herself up on her tiny sofa every time he stayed with her.

Anthony Morgan nodded at her. 'Yes. That's all done for you. I should tell you that, believe it or not, I'm retiring at the end of this month, so if there is anything further you'd like me to do for you, I suggest you act quickly.'

'You're retiring? Good for you! It's about time.'

But Anthony waved a dismissive hand. 'I predict I'll be dead before the end of the year. That's the problem when you stop. A word of advice, Mrs Elliott, don't ever stop!'

She smiled back at him. 'Don't you worry, Anthony. I don't intend to.' She walked to the office door, placed her hand on the handle, and paused. 'Actually, there is one more thing that I'd like you to do for me.'

Branwell was leaning up the side of the building when Edith emerged from the solicitor's office.

'Thank God for that,' he said. 'I've been freezing my tits off for ages waiting for you. I thought you said that it was a quick signature.'

'It was,' replied Edith. 'Did you know that Anthony was retiring?'

'Blimey! Anthony? Retiring? Well, that's certainly surprised me. He'll be dead within a month,' said Branwell nonchalantly.

'He's given himself until the end of the year,' replied Edith.

Branwell frowned. 'A little optimistic if you ask me. Still, if it makes him feel better, let him think that.'

They trundled arm in arm down the street in silence. They were meeting Simon and Emma in the restaurant around the corner for a celebratory meal and drink following Sarah's conviction. Although, celebrating her friend's demise and thirty-year prison sentence seemed too unfeeling for Edith. Was she happy she'd worked out who murdered Harry and Winston? Absolutely. But it had come at a heavy price for her to pay, even with all of her millions in the bank. She'd happily give every last penny away just to have been proven wrong, but sadly, that wasn't to be. How different life could have been for Sarah if she'd told Edith that day at the cricket match what Harry had done to her? Edith would have done everything in her power to help her friend, and failing that, she would have certainly ensured that Sarah didn't suffer financially. But Sarah, in her own muddle-headed way, had thought that murder had been her only option of revenge. It was such a sorry waste of the limited life she had left.

Edith's new-found friendship with Simon and Emma had brought some comfort. Granted, they weren't beating down her door, begging for help with the new investigations that landed on their desks, but they did ask for her opinion from time to time. It was also nice that they allowed her and Branwell to refer to them by their Christian names rather than their formal police titles. However, Simon had flatly vetoed Branwell's Crimewatchers name. You couldn't have everything, she supposed.

'Are you okay, sister dearest?' asked Branwell as they walked. 'You've been extremely quiet recently.'

Edith sighed. He was right, of course, as Branwell always was. She still hadn't told him about the brain aneurysm, believing that the timing just wasn't right: He was too drunk. She was too drunk. They'd booked a holiday. Christmas was coming up. But the reality was she was scared, not about his reaction, but how he might treat her differently if he knew. Branwell would molly-coddle Edith; that was his way. But Edith didn't want him to do that. She didn't want pity from her brother. She just wanted him to be him – that beautifully arrogant, unthinking soul that was.

'It's just all this hoo-hah with Sarah now that she's been sentenced,' she replied, only partially lying.

'So long as you're not holding anything back, then that's allowed,' he told her. 'But while we're on the subject, there is something that I've been keeping from you.'

'Oh?' she said, looking up at him with concern.

Please, God, don't let him tell her that he's dying. Not now she's only just gotten him back.

Branwell removed his arm from hers and reached into the inside of his suit jacket, pulling out a yellowing envelope.

'Just don't be mad at me,' he said as he handed it over. 'There never seemed to be the right time to show you.'

Edith turned the envelope over, recognising the elegant handwriting immediately.

'I found it amongst father's private papers in his study after he died,' said Branwell. 'In truth, I didn't know what to do with it. I almost told you back when we first reconciled. Do you remember? We were walking back to your flat, but then Sarah was outside.'

With shaking hands, Edith removed the letter inside and began reading.

My darling children,

I write this with the heaviest of hearts. It is no longer possible for me to stay with your father. You're old enough to understand just how much of a brute he is and how, with each blow he delivers, a part of my soul feels like it is breaking away. If I stay, I know without question that eventually, my soul will be too shattered to glue back together. I have remained living this existence for only two reasons, and that is because of you both. You have been the only light on my darkest of days, and without you, I feel I would have crumbled such a long time ago.

But seeing you both making your own way in the world has made me realise that you have little need of me at the hall any longer. I am leaving, but I must be clear that I am not leaving you. I have secured accommodation some distance away, and when the time is right, I shall return, and you will have the choice as to whether or not you wish to join me when I do.

My heart will forever belong to you both, and I pray that you will not be too angry at me for leaving without you, if only temporarily, as either way it is too long a wait. I shall be back by Spring, so please keep a weathered eye out for me.

Forever your loving mother

Edith reread the letter, unable to tear her eyes away from her first contact with her mother in over fifty years. She'd always known that she'd left her father, but the fact that she had never returned or contacted Edith and Branwell had been like a knife slicing her heart. And yet, here in her hands was the proof that she was always intended to come home for them.

'And this was in father's things?' she asked, astounded.

Branwell nodded. 'Tucked away in a copy of Shakespeare's *The Winter's Tale*, no less. Tell me – what was your first thought when reading that? The first thing to jump out and slap you across the face?'

'Father found the letter. Mother never returned. I don't think she ever escaped,' said Edith.

Branwell took a deep breath and nodded his head. 'Exactly what I thought, too, Edie. So it begs the question, if she never left, then what happened to her?'

Edith's senses were running wild. Her imagination was throwing up new images and scenarios: her father's furious face upon reading the letter and her mother's terrified screams as he confronted her. And then there was blackness—an empty void of nothingness waiting for more details that her logical brain craved to make sense of it all.

There was pounding on the window, making them both jump. Simon was in the window of the restaurant across the road, motioning them to come inside with his hand before making exaggerated gestures of rubbing his stomach and looking at an imaginary watch on his wrist.

Edith carefully folded the letter and handed it back to Branwell.

'You know who this is a case for?' he said, wiggling the envelope at her.

'Please, Branwell. Don't say it,' begged Edith.

'It's a case for the Crimewatchers,' and she let out a loud groan.

Even at these most distressing moments, he still had the knack for making her smile, no matter how difficult it felt.

'Come on, I'll weaken them by plying them both with bottles of champagne and then it s time for you to turn on the charm. They'll have a case opened by the end of the week,' he continued, dragging Edith inside.

Chapter Thirty Four

'It's strange how things work out, isn't Ronnie? Six months ago, I was a different person entirely, coasting through life as though it had no meaning whatsoever.'

Edith moved Ronnie to the coffee table. This was a serious face-to-face conversation, not one that could be had if she was looking up at the mantlepiece.

'I was never one to believe in divine intervention, but it does make you think sometimes when life throws you a curveball, quite literally in my case, and it veers you off on a whole new trajectory. Had Harry not knocked me out with that cricket ball, I would never have been taken to hospital and found out that I had a brain aneurysm. Had that not happened, I wouldn't have decided to go and see

Anthony Morgan and claim my inheritance. If I had not claimed the inheritance, Anthony would never have told Bramwell where I lived. And had Branwell not come back into my life, I would never have attempted to solve the murders without his support – well, without his nagging at any rate.'

She'd become more philosophical of late, viewing everything that had happened to her as though, like in the murder investigation, somebody was guiding her on the right path. At first, she'd thought maybe it was Ronnie helping her along from his heavenly pub in the clouds, but then she reminded herself that this was Ronnie she was talking about. Firstly, she had to seriously consider whether he even made it up there, given the type of man that he'd been, and secondly, even if he had managed to find his way through those pearly gates, what would be the chances of him helping her do something that she'd always wanted to do? Pretty bloody unlikely.

Well, whoever was helping her along, Edith was grateful to them because, for the first time in her life, she felt as though she was the person she was always meant to be. It had stung a little that it had come so late in life, but something was better than nothing, she supposed.

'You're changing the subject, Ron. I don't want to talk about that right now,' she told the urn sternly. 'I'm still unsure what to do about the whole thing. It feels like I'll be opening up Pandora's box with that one. Branwell's keen to look into it. He even spoke to Emma and Simon about it all while I sat there and listened in silence like a complete idiot. What did you say? No, Emma and Simon agree with him. They think it's completely fishy; I suppose they have the noses to know when something isn't quite right. I'll let it all sink in first and then decide after I've had a good think about it.'

She sighed and leaned back in the armchair, looking around her almost empty flat. A few boxes remained for the moving company to pick up tomorrow, but everything else, apart from the armchair, had already been taken to the new house.

'What I wanted to talk about was what will happen after today. Now, I know you won't like it, but I think it's best that we say our goodbyes.'

The googly eyes stared back at Edith.

'Don't be like that, Ron. Branwell thinks I'm completely doolally talking to you the way I do, but the simple fact is that you're not here anymore. I talked to you because I was so used to you being around that when you went, it felt as though my whole identity had been stripped away from me. It was always Edie and Ron; that's how people used to view us – as one person but moulded into two different bodies. I was lost without you. I couldn't function, and I just couldn't let you go. But now, moving away from this flat and to somewhere different feels like I'm starting anew. Let's not be sad about it all, though. I've been thinking about where to sprinkle you.'

It had been difficult trying to find somewhere suitable, if Edith was being honest. Ronnie had liked so few places in the village unless they sold alcohol, but seeing as none of the local pubs would allow her to sprinkle his ashes on their carpets, she was limited in where she could take him. Even Brian Marston said no to her, which was a bit of a cheek really, considering she'd cleared their names from a murder inquiry. They'd better hope that they didn't need her help with anything else in the future because it'd be a solid pass from her.

'I thought you might like the village green. It's close to the pub for a start, and in a way, it's where everything changed for me; it's where I became my own person again. No – no arguments. I'm sorry, Ronnie, but it has to be done. And it's happening now before I change my mind.'

She rose sharply from the armchair and grabbed the urn. 'I know you don't like the dark, but it won't be for long,' she said as she placed the urn into her bag.

Edith slid on her coat and headed out of the door with Ronnie. This would be their last walk together. The sun hung low in the sky, casting long shadows on the pavements. As Edith looked down at hers, she smiled as she realised that, for once, it was Ronnie who was in her shadow and not the other way around.

She rounded the corner and walked past the small row of shops, and as she was about to cross the road to head towards the green, she heard the soft jangle of the café bell, and she turned to see Felicity hurrying towards her.

'Edith,' she said as she dashed to her side. 'How's the move going?'

'Good. I'm almost there,' she said. 'How are you, Felicity? Well, I hope?'

Felicity grabbed Edith's arm and pulled her closer to her. 'Well? I'm over the bloody moon. I just had to tell somebody. Last week, the police called to say that with the investigation over and closed, they'll be returning my money before the end of the month. And then, just when I thought things couldn't get any better, I had a visit from one of those inheritance firms. You know, the ones where they hunt down long-lost relatives of somebody who's died without making a will. Well, apparently, I had this great-aunt who emigrated to Canada. And blow me, I've only gone and inherited one hundred thousand pounds!'

Edith's mouth dropped open. 'Felicity! That's wonderful news.'

'I know! I just can't believe it. It means that I can keep this place now, and hopefully, if I spend it wisely, it should see me through for a long time.'

'It couldn't have happened to a nicer person,' said Edith, squeezing the woman's hand. 'Congratulations. And I'm so happy you get to keep the café now.'

'Oh, me too. I couldn't imagine leaving this old thing behind. You know what it's like when something's been with you for a long time; it'd feel like losing an arm or a leg. Without it, I wouldn't know what to do with myself.'

Edith felt a familiar pang in her stomach.

'Anyway, I must dash. The solicitor is still inside, and he wants to make sure all of the paperwork is finalised before he leaves.'

Felicity gave an excited wave to Edith and dashed back inside the café. Edith watched her go, and as the door closed, her eyes drifted over to the window and to Anthony Morgan, who was sitting inside eating a large slice of chocolate cake. He smiled at Edith, raising his coffee cup in the air to her, and Edith discreetly waved back at him before turning back to face the road. But Felicity's words echoed in her mind, preventing her from taking that next step off the pavement.

'I suppose I should at least take you to the new house to show you what it's like,' said Edith, squeezing the urn through the bag tucked under her shoulder.

She turned away from the road and started the short walk to her new house, where Branwell and Dickens were already waiting for her.

'But listen, if you start playing up, then I won't even bother taking you to the green; I'll flush you straight down the toilet instead, so you'd better behave.'

About the author

Jayne Bailey lives in the sunny climate of Birmingham, UK. A prolific writer, she's written over a hundred books in several different genres and shows no signs of slowing down. As a massive fan of cosy crime, it came as no surprise that Jayne embarked on her latest creation, Edith Elliott, who she named after her beloved grandmother, Edith, who was every bit as astute and shrewd as her namesake.

If you'd like to contact Jayne, you can email her at jaynebaileyauthor@gmail.com. Jayne loves to hear from her readers and always endeavours to respond as quickly as possible.

If you enjoyed this book, feel free to follow Jayne on Amazon, where you'll be notified of any future releases.

Coming Soon!

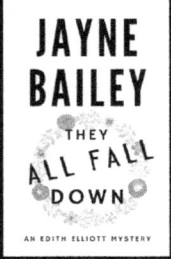

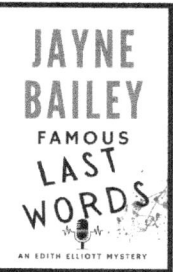

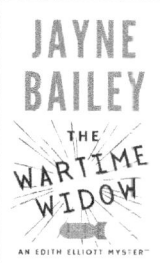

Printed in Great Britain
by Amazon